The Stranger at the Door
Paperback Copyright © 2022 Lorhainne Ekelund
Editor: Talia Leduc

All rights reserved.
ISBN-13: 978-1990590221

Give feedback on the book at:
lorhainneeckhart@hotmail.com

Twitter: @LEckhart
Facebook: AuthorLorhainneEckhart

Printed in the U.S.A

THE STRANGER AT THE DOOR

Billy Jo McCabe Mystery

LORHAINNE ECKHART

Billy Jo McCabe wants only to help children over-come their troubled lives, as she herself struggles to forget the childhood nightmare she survived. She took sociology and prelaw at the insistence of her adoptive father, Chase McCabe, and learned how to use power tools from her adoptive mother, Rose. She loves reading in the backs of bookstores before tucking the book back on the shelf and slipping out without paying. She has a fondness for peanut butter and dill pickle sandwiches, has a three-legged cat named Harley, hates running (because that was all she did as a kid), and secretly binges on brownies and red wine on the sofa in front of her TV every Friday night.

She's never been married and has dated only twice. She visits Chase and Rose when summoned and shows up dutifully for every holiday with her family, but she has no siblings to speak of, and she feels a growing resentment for the mother who abandoned her in foster care. Despite proudly maintaining the same prickly attitude that nearly landed her behind bars as a kid, she has yet to speak up to Chase, who interferes in her life too frequently, ready to fix every problem, whether she wants him to or not.

One thing no one knows about Billy Jo is that she moved to Roche Harbor because it's the only clue she has about the last known whereabouts of the woman who abandoned her.

The Cop

Mark Friessen, son of Jed and Diana Friessen, has landed accidently in the role of small-town detective, a position in which he's going nowhere. Nearly married once, and broken-hearted three times, he's sworn he'll stay single forever, and he keeps his tattoo of a former girlfriend as a reminder that only fools fall in love. He's tall, attractive, and stubborn, and he refuses to live in the shadow of his two older brothers, Chris and Danny.

As Roche Harbor's youngest detective, he sleeps with a gun under his pillow. He has a stray dog that won't leave, and he swears that the only two food groups that exist are meat and potatoes. His favorite drink is black coffee in the morning, sugared coffee in the afternoon, and a shot of whiskey in his coffee at night to keep him warm.

***Each book in this series is a complete book, with no cliff-hangers, and can be read as a standalone. However, these books may contain references to situations from earlier books in the series. As with any long book series that focuses on specific char-acters, their changing relationships, and how their lives continue to unfold, you may find it more enjoyable to read the series in order of publishing, as there will be developments and changes in the relationship dynamics of the core characters.*

She knocked on his door. He never should have answered.

As newly appointed chief of police, Mark Friessen is settling into his small-town role when he uncovers the twisted tale of a woman forced to marry the man who killed her family.

When the woman goes looking for help, knocking on his door, Mark and Billy Jo are thrust into a web of lies that tests their own complex relationship, as they discover secrets in the couple's shadowy past that could drive a wedge between them for good.

Mark and Billy Jo are continuing to learn the hard way that stepping on the wrong toes could have serious consequences. Thrown into the center of a dangerous and bizarre case, they have to face their own doubts about each other, and soon, they may wish this woman had never knocked on Mark's door.

Chapter 1

"You given any thought to redoing this office and really making it yours? You know, putting your own stamp on it?" Billy Jo was sitting in a padded old chair, her bare feet in flip-flops up on his desk, and he thought she wore pink nail polish on her toes. Something about the bellbottom blue jeans and light peach blouse she wore, which even hinted that she was a girl, had him wondering what was different about her as of late.

He looked around the glassed-in office, with its old desk covered in papers and files, the cabinet behind him, and the computer, and he gestured from where he lounged in the black swivel chair, which had once been the chief's. "It's just an office, Billy Jo, and it is mine. I don't need anything fancy."

She shot him a look from across the desk, where she seemed to fit so well, lounging. They had settled into a routine that was both welcome and expected, with her stopping in after work every day. "Well, at least paint it," she said. "What are all those plaques up there on the wall? Is that a baseball back there? And those old photos, Mark, you've got to take those down." She gestured to them, unsmiling. This was the snarky side of Billy Jo that came out when she had something to say.

He had to fight the urge to smile. She was so familiar. He didn't turn around to see the black and white photos on the wall of the young chief, then a new cop, standing with the old chief he'd later replaced and the council. He'd personally never met any of them. He stood up and reached for one, seeing a smile on the face of the old chief, one he never remembered seeing, and looked over to Billy Jo, taking in her blue eyes. He was doing his damnedest to figure out where to tread with her and how this thing he couldn't put a name to worked between them.

"Fine. I'll box this up, but I'm not painting. You want to do it, be my guest. Since you're just sitting there, take a look at these." He reached for a pile of applications and resumes for the new deputy position and dumped them on the desk in front of her with a *thunk*. In the bullpen outside, Carmen, who wore blue jeans and a faded black T-shirt, was really pulling double duty since they were down to just the two of them. He missed having Gail to answer the phones and do all she had done to keep the station running.

"So what are these?" Billy Jo reached for the pile of papers as she dropped her feet to the ground.

He realized, as he looked at her brown hair, that it

appeared the layers had been freshly cut. Something about her seemed so different, so not the girl hiding behind frumpy clothes. He walked around the desk, watching the way she thumbed through the papers, the way her brow knit when she was focused, reading and absorbing something, the way she never hesitated to jump in. She was so damn smart that her opinion on everything mattered to him more than he could have explained to anyone.

"Resumes, applications for the deputy job, someone to answer the phones and do everything Gail did. The top of the pile there was sent over by the council, and see all the ones with a red star marked on top? The council has pretty much ordered me to hire one of them. The ones on the bottom are the ones I found and came across."

She flicked those blue eyes up to him, reading between the lines and knowing what he was thinking without him having to say another word. This was the comfortable relationship they were morphing into.

He kept walking out the open door and over to the corner by Gail's old desk, where a few boxes were stacked for recycling. He took in Lucky, who was curled up, asleep, before he reached for a box and walked back across the bullpen. Carmen was hanging up the phone, and her chair squeaked as she stretched and started closing up files. She lifted her gaze to him, her wary dark eyes tracking him, and he found himself stopping beside her desk.

"You get today's report finished?" he said.

She opened her laptop without a word and

gestured to the screen as if she expected him to check her work. He didn't look at her screen, not pulling his gaze from her, still holding the box and waiting, so she pulled in a breath and said, "Was about to email it to you. Theft at the pharmacy of a bunch of back-to-school supplies, some drinking in the park, public indecency, and a lot of nuisance crap that would seem to indicate an alarming rise, except it seems most troublemakers were used to the times Chief Shephard had me run the same route, so that tells me everyone had their watches set to when I would be making the rounds like clockwork, and it was only the idiots who were getting caught. Now I can't drive anywhere without seeing something, and there isn't enough of me going around to do anything. Then there are all the noise complaints, parties, loud music, neighbors fighting, and the bylaw crap still tossed this way, from illegal camping to people living in their cars, and where am I supposed to tell them to go?"

He could see her frustration. "Do what you can. It's a judgement call. Send me the report, and I'll see what I can take off your plate until I get a deputy hired in here."

She sat up and swiveled her chair around. "Well, won't be soon enough for me, Mark—sorry, Chief."

There was something odd about being called Chief. He wondered if he'd ever get used to it.

"Clock out and go have some dinner," he said. "I'm going to be here awhile yet."

Carmen yanked her desk drawer open and pulled out her keys, and Mark walked back to his office, where Billy Jo was reading through the stack of applications. Damn, she was too perfect. He had to remind himself how easily he could sabotage the good things in his life.

"You look nice, in case I forgot to mention it," he said as he rested the box on his desk. "You did something new with your hair."

She suddenly stilled. Right, she didn't take compliments at all. From the way she flicked those sharp blue eyes to him, he could tell she was uncomfortable, and he waited for her to toss something snarky his way.

"Here. You picked the ones on the bottom?" she said. Okay, so she was going to ignore the compliment. That was one way not to handle it. She pulled out two papers and held them out to him, and he reached for them, seeing two names, Mike Schneider and Georgette Hunter.

"That was quick," he said. "Why these two and not the starred ones favored by the council?"

She neatened the pile of papers and then leaned back in the chair, balancing them on her lap. "Well, for one, it would take a fool not to see that of the council picks, most are either their friends or relatives or, as with these first two, have more experience than you, so the council is likely looking for your replacement, someone who is going to do exactly what they say, report to them, and take all their directions directly. I happen to know that after every weekly meeting you have with the councillors, a few of them criticize you, complaining and commenting that you're going to ruin the policing on the island."

He stared at her as he pulled the black and whites off the wall and tucked them into the box. "Excuse me?" he said. What was she hearing that he wasn't? She didn't even smile, and he could see she was dead serious. "Are you shitting me? Who in all hell is talking out of turn? What goes on in the council is confidential, yet now you're telling me…"

"You're stepping on toes, Mark."

He straightened and could feel the alpha fighting inside him. His first instinct as he took in the seriousness staring back at him was to walk out the door and knock on the door of the head of council, Mary Jane Trundell, or maybe Hal Green or Herb Walker, so he could go toe to toe with them and find out what the fuck they thought they were doing, sharing anything about what went on in the council.

"I can tell by your face that you're ready to go a round with one or all of them," she said, "but that would be a mistake. I'm not sure how many are furious, but I know Herb Walker has been the most vocal, and I heard Hal Green was talking about how you don't play ball with the Rotary Club. Several have said Mary Jane isn't happy with you and the fact that you're going all cowboy with your policing." She lifted the stack and settled them on his desk as she leaned forward.

His jaw slackened as he rested both hands on the edge of the box and squeezed, then lifted his hand and dragged it over his jaw roughly. "Are you sure?

They said I was a cowboy, seriously? Is that because I outright refused to allow the council to dictate to me which crimes to ignore and which to put my focus on? Did you know we currently have more than three dozen people sleeping in their cars on the island because they can't put a roof over their head? The council has ordered me to make sure they know they can't park anywhere overnight, which means basically kicking them off the island.

"Then we had three driving without a license. One was a young mother who couldn't have afforded bail or the license renewal fee, and I knew that, so I let her off with a warning and told her to park and pay the fee, but the council ordered me to charge her and lock her up. If I do, she won't get out until she goes before a judge, and then she'll be hit with another fine she won't be able to afford, so she'll still be locked up, and her kids will be tossed in the social services system.

"Of the other two I stopped, one shithead had lost his license for driving two times over the legal limit, and he refused a breathalyzer, yet his lawyer had him out before the ink was dry, citing that he was on pain meds and wasn't drinking. That was a load of crap, considering the alcohol on his breath could have knocked me over. He just so happens to be a cousin of Herb Walker.

"The other was a snotnosed teenager who took his mom's BMW for a joy ride. The family is from Seattle, and the dad is some tech giant with a summer home here worth millions. You know that kid laughed when Carmen pulled him over? He'd almost run down an elderly woman on one of those mobility scooters. When Carmen yanked him out of the car, he screamed at her to keep her dirty half-breed hands off him and said his dad would make sure she was fired and would pay for it."

Billy Jo said nothing. Mark had refused to back down when it came to how the council felt they could tell him to police this island: kid gloves with some and paramilitary tactics with others.

"Yeah, I heard about that too," she said with a hint of a smile. "Wasn't it Mary Jane whose phone was ringing with a call from the dad, who apparently contributed largely to her campaign? He threatened that he had enough clout to redirect infrastructure funding from the island to another region and halt the upgrade of the water treatment plant, meaning the tax bills of every full-time island resident would be hiked to cover the cost. That would get Mary Jane voted out, so I heard she folded like a deck of cards under the pressure. And you did what?"

"I charged the privileged little shit," he said, "although it didn't do any good. The DA has already thrown it out, calling me and chewing out my ass. But I made it clear to good old dad, who showed up here, breathing down my neck, that he's to keep his kid off the island, and if ever again we have a problem with him, a video of his racist diatribe will be all over the news."

She lifted her brows, leaned back, and crossed her

feet on his desk, and he wasn't sure if she was amused. "You have a video?"

He reached for the baseball and the plaques and shoved them in the box. "No, but he doesn't know that. Anyway, I ordered a body camera for Carmen, and she'll wear it. The council will freak, mind you, when they get the bill, but I'm not having her credibility shredded because of some privileged kid who gets a free ride and thinks he can do anything he wants without consequence. Because her word won't count against his if shit hits the fan." He knew he was shoving everything in the box a little harder than necessary. "As far as Hal Green, I reminded him of all the tickets he had the chief write off for him over the years and let him know I have a copy of every one of them, including his emails to the chief telling him to take care of it."

Her expression was unreadable. "I thought you didn't keep any of the chief's insurance, the dirt he had on the council," she said. "You said you didn't want to operate that way."

Mark shrugged, thinking of the files in the bottom drawer, the proof of how Herb Walker had dipped into the funding for the island homeless, the tickets for Hal Green, and the photos of the head of the council herself, Mary Jane, with Philip Maddox, the reason the chief was no longer the chief. "If those running things actually played by the rules, I guess you and I wouldn't be having this conversation," he replied. "Didn't say I would use them, but I'd be stupid to throw them out."

She nodded. "Heard you eventually paid the license renewal fee for Grace Peters, too," she said. "Word gets around that you can't help being a good guy, Mark."

He only grunted. Aggressive prosecution against a woman who just couldn't afford her license didn't sit right with him. "She's got kids, no support, and her job barely pays her a living wage."

Billy Jo lifted her hands. "Hey, you don't need to justify it to me. I get it, Mark, and I'm behind you. I'm just saying that the council doesn't like being backed into a corner, and they especially don't like having a chief they can't control, so you'll need to watch your back. Now, those two, you should call them." She gestured to the two resumes she'd pulled out, Georgette Walker and Mike Schneider. One was from Salem, the other from Olympia. "And I'm starving, so how much more do you have to do?"

He took in the box, the girl, and the resumes on his desk. "Tons, but it'll keep." He reached for the pile of resumes and tossed them on top of the box. "For dinner, how about steak?"

She shrugged and stood up. "You're cooking?" She reached for her bag, and he took in the curves she was no longer hiding.

"Yeah. I'll throw steaks on the grill, and you can go through the rest of these resumes…" He lifted the box and started out of his office, following her.

"And the box?" She gestured back to him as he flicked off the light with his elbow and whistled to Lucky, who was now up and striding to the door.

"I'll drop it off at the chief's," he said. "As you pointed out, these are his things."

She pulled open the door.

"Lock it, will you?" he said. "The keys are in my pocket."

She hesitated only a second before reaching into his pocket, a touch he hadn't expected, and she pulled the keys out. He strode to his Jeep and opened the back to stuff the box in, then grabbed the papers and pulled open the front door.

Billy Jo tossed him the keys, which he caught one-handed, before starting to her new Nissan Rogue. She would just follow him to his place, he knew, and he considered for a second this relationship they'd fallen into. Her place or his place didn't matter. It was always dinner, talking, and then he or she would leave. Maybe tonight he could figure out a way to change her mind and get her to stay.

Chapter 2

Mark turned the steaks on the grill and sprinkled on more seasoning. Billy Jo was carrying on a conversation with Lucky, and he couldn't help smiling at how his dog listened more to her than him at times.

"Here, put this on and heat it up," Billy Jo said, handing him a small skillet with broccoli and butter to sauté. He wondered where that had come from, but then, his fridge seemed to be stocked more and more with real food he knew she was responsible for. "Those potatoes done?"

He used the tongs to turn two baked potatoes wrapped in tin foil. Cooking was something he didn't normally do, and all he could think was that his domestication had come out of nowhere. "Should be. So, you give any thought to what we talked about?"

She stood right beside him, and he looked down at her, taking in how cute she was. She never flirted with him, ever, and he didn't think she'd even know how if she tried. She just stared at him and gestured to the broccoli sizzling in the butter. "Don't let that burn."

He flipped the broccoli and moved it around the frypan on the grill. She was still standing there. "You know, Billy Jo, it's not lost on me that when you're uncomfortable about something, you just don't want to talk. You're about the worst when it comes to talking things through. Instead, you ignore me and say nothing. But this, with us, only works if you talk."

She pulled her arms over her chest. "You get that tattoo scheduled to be removed yet? Because I told you I don't want to be looking at your ex-girlfriend every time you take off that shirt." There she went, changing the subject again.

"You know, Lucky and Harley will get along great," he said. "You've seen them when he's at your place, no fights... I'm thinking this is more about your comfort level. Harley would do great over here with Lucky. Look at all the outdoors he'd have to wander..."

She was still looking up at him, breathing in and out, her chest rising. "He's a three-legged cat. He doesn't wander outside. He stays inside or sits on my deck. He couldn't protect himself if he wandered. You want a beer?"

She was already walking back into his small one-bedroom cabin. He gestured after her with his tongs, fighting the urge to wrap his hands around her neck. She was the only woman he found himself completely off kilter with, unable to reason with.

"Opinionated, stubborn, difficult…" he said under his breath, maybe because she still hadn't answered him. He wondered if this was where guys learned to toe the line.

"Mark!" she called out to him, holding up a beer from the open fridge.

He gestured with a sweep of his tongs. "Nope. Carmen isn't on call tonight, and I'm not about to give the council any reason to bounce me."

She shoved the beer back into his dated old fridge with a clatter. "Then how about water, or do you want this lonely can of orange soda?" she called out.

"Nothing, I'm good." He shook his head, flipped the steaks again, and turned off the grill as Billy Jo walked his way with an empty plate and a glass of wine. She handed the plate to him in comfortable silence. She seemed to just know what he needed, and it left him wondering why they were still dancing around each other. He was trying to figure out how to navigate this maze, treading carefully, recalling his history of screwing up every good thing he'd had.

"So can we talk about how you avoid answering by changing the subject? I'm serious, Billy Jo…" He let out a rough laugh, trying to dial back his frustration. "You know how I feel about you. Is it about this place, sex, or what? I feel like I'm having to force the conversation when I would rather not talk, but if I don't, seriously, I'm starting to think dancing around is all we'll ever do. Are you scared of me, of this between us? Is that why I feel as if you're one step forward and two back all the time? And don't think I haven't noticed your subtle change from baggy comfortable clothes to looking more like a girl."

He took the plate from her a little harder than he meant to, and she narrowed her eyes, her mouth tight, her posture stiff. He put the steaks and baked potatoes on the plate and reached for the hot skillet using the mitt Billy Jo had held out without a word. He shook his head as he walked around her with dinner, seeing how she held the wineglass, still saying nothing.

He stopped beside her and leaned down, so close. "And here you go again, suddenly mute."

She flicked her gaze up to him and let out a frustrated breath, and he made himself keep moving because he could feel the edge of her anger. He would gladly have reached out and shaken her if he thought it would do any good.

"Frustrating…. Like, what the hell am I doing?" he said under his breath as he put the plate down with a clatter and set the skillet on the stove. He rested his hands on the counter and gave his head a shake before reaching for two plates on the open shelf, which he realized had never looked this neat and organized.

He heard the door close and sensed her walking his way, so he held out a plate to her as she appeared quietly beside him and put her glass of wine down.

"Just FYI, I'm not scared of you, Mark," she said. "It's me I'm scared of. You want to have this conversation, then fine, let's have it. We're friends…"

"We're more than friends and you know it," he snapped, cutting her off, forking one of the steaks onto a plate. She rolled her shoulders as he reached for a baked potato and unwrapped the tinfoil.

"So we're dating," she said.

"Not dating, either. Dating is getting to know someone, testing the waters to see if a committed relationship is possible. I told you I'm not dating. You got under my skin. This, here, is dancing around, and that's all you, baby." He knew he sounded like an asshole, but he was tired of this, and he wondered when he'd found himself seeing her as the one.

"I'm not afraid of sleeping with you, Mark, or sex, so let's get that straight. But you have issues, one of which is the tattoo of your former girlfriend that you should have removed by now. So let's talk about dancing around, shall we?"

"I called and booked an appointment for a week Thursday, but it has to be done on the mainland, and that's if I have a new deputy trained and here to help Carmen so I can leave the island. So no, I haven't blown it off, but with the shitstorm that went on here with the chief and me taking over, you know I can't just hop on a ferry and leave right now."

He had her backed against the counter, so close to her that he settled his hands on either side of her so she couldn't move. She looked to one side and then the other until she was forced to look at him. He knew he was in her space, touching her, pushing her. He could feel the pull of her breath, see the way she reacted to him.

"You really booked it?" she said.

He angled his head without stepping back, and

she flicked her gaze to his lips. He didn't wait for her to say yes before he leaned in and pressed a kiss to her lips, easy, soft, and let it linger. Her hand on his arm traced the skin up to the edge of his faded T-shirt, and he settled his hand on her hip, over the curve of her waist, and up her back, then slipped his arm around her and pulled her right against him as he deepened the kiss.

She pressed against his chest but didn't push him away. It was instinctive and natural as he lifted her, resting her on the edge of the counter, pressing a kiss to her neck, the soft skin at the V of her open blouse, and he heard her hiss. Just then, the dog barked, and Mark jumped. There was a knock at the door.

He pulled back, still holding her as she slid down, mourning the interruption, the loss. He stepped away, his hand on her for another second, and he angled his head, unsure what was staring back at him.

"Dammit, always something." He hadn't meant to say it out loud. "Lucky, come here!" he called out as the dog barked again. He made himself take one step and another, glancing once to his open bedroom door and his holstered gun sitting on the dresser.

He walked to the door and pulled it open to see a woman with light hair, slender, wearing a loose blouse. "Hi, are you lost?" he said, taking her in. He figured she had to be about five foot five, maybe—young, pretty.

"So sorry. You're the chief, right?" she said.

He didn't step back, feeling uncomfortable. The young woman looked up at him, and he couldn't help being a little pissed. Billy Jo stepped up behind him, and he set a hand on her arm. "Sorry, can I help you?" he said before pulling in a rattled breath.

He'd been so into Billy Jo, that kiss, and having her one step from under him, that he hadn't heard a stranger arrive. He stepped away from Billy Jo, his hand lingering a second on her to keep her behind him, maybe from the fear of everything that had happened around him.

"Are you the chief?" she said, her voice soft. She appeared in her early twenties, if that.

"I am. And you are?" he replied. Lucky was growling behind him, and he turned back to the dog, seeing Billy Jo with her arms crossed, looking intently at the woman. Lucky growled and barked again. "Lucky, come over here," he said. "Billy Jo, can you…?"

He didn't have to say any more, as Lucky warily came over to him, and he grabbed the collar Billy Jo had bought for him and pulled him back. Billy Jo reached for him, making him sit, as Mark took in the open door to his bedroom and the gun still sitting on the dresser. He didn't know why he was feeling so on edge.

He stepped closer, standing in the open door right in front of the woman, and he could hear Billy Jo talking to his dog behind him. Her expression was off, maybe from the way the dog had reacted to her.

"You didn't tell me who you are. Is this a police matter?" he said. "Your coming out here is unusual. We're kind of in a crunch right now with staffing down. I haven't been on the island that long, so I haven't had a chance to get to know everyone." He gestured to her, looking over her head to see a sleek silver Jaguar Coupe, likely why he hadn't heard her pull in.

She squeezed the silver chain strap of her purse over her shoulder, her mouth tight. "I apologize for intruding, and yes, I hesitated in coming to you. In fact, I've sat outside the station—well, just on the road, with plans to walk in and talk to you, but I'm afraid I chickened out. I didn't want anyone to see me, because then there would be talk, and then he'd know."

Her eyes were deep blue, and Mark found himself lifting his hand to invite her inside. "Okay, come in. Why don't you have a seat?" He gestured to the old leather sectional and glanced back to Billy Jo, shooting her a puzzled look. She didn't let go of Lucky, who, he realized, wasn't letting the woman out of his sight. He couldn't remember ever seeing his dog act that way: wary, watchful. *Hmm.*

She took a step inside and over to the sofa, running her slender hands over her deep blue jeans. She wore makeup, thick mascara, and her lips were full. Her identity was still a mystery.

"So why don't we start with your name?" he said, his hands going to his hips.

The woman seemed to track him with just her eyes. "And it won't get back to my husband?"

He made himself shake his head. "This is just us

here. I can't help you unless you tell me what it is. Are you in trouble, scared? What is it?"

Odd, he thought as she nodded, glancing past him to Billy Jo before looking back at him.

"My name is Sunday, and I'm not sure where to start. Did you know child marriages are legal in this country? I'm not old enough to vote, buy a house, join the military, or drink alcohol, but I've been married for three years."

He didn't have to look to know that Billy Jo was now standing beside him, and Lucky's nails scratched on the old hardwood as he lay down behind him.

"You're married. How old are you?"

"I'm sixteen, old enough to drive now. I have two children, my first when I was fourteen, the second when I was fifteen. When I had my babies, the hospital knew, and the school I went to knew, and the courts knew where I was married before a judge."

Billy Jo hissed beside him, or maybe it was the sound in his own head. He knew he was staring like a fool, trying to wrap his head around what she was saying. Maybe that was why the woman opened her purse, pulled out her wallet and driver's license, and held it out to him.

He found himself staring at her before reaching for the license, seeing a photo of a woman free of makeup, appearing much like a young girl. He took in the year, the birthdate, and the name Sunday Byrd, then flicked his gaze right back to her. The makeup she wore made her look older. Yeah, there it was, the same image. He could see it now, how young she was.

He held the license out to Billy Jo and let her take it, maybe because he didn't know where to begin.

"I can see by your face that either you don't believe me or you're having trouble wrapping your head around this," Sunday said.

Billy Jo tensed beside him, and he dragged his hand over his face. He couldn't figure out what to say, because he knew that her being married, as sick as it was, was legal in too many places.

"Is that why you're here?" he said.

She shook her head. "No, I'm here because the man I was forced to marry killed my family."

Chapter 3

"Could you excuse us a second?" Billy Jo said, still holding the license. She dragged her gaze over to Mark, who appeared tense and quiet. She was beginning to read him so well, his many moods, right down to the way he had to fight the urge to wrap his hands around her neck when she went toe to toe with him and stepped on his male ego—though, to his credit, he had a restraint she hadn't expected. Then there was the way he became quiet when he was completely rattled and thrown, like now. She reached for his bare arm, feeling the warmth, the strength, and pulled.

"What are you doing?" he said, but he went along with her, letting her lead him and the dog, whom she grabbed by the collar and shooed into the bedroom, where he jumped onto the unmade bed.

She glanced back once from the bedroom to Sunday, who was sitting on the sofa, staring at her, saying nothing. "We'll be right back," Billy Jo said before closing the door.

Mark paced, unsettled, and dragged his hand over his face, likely still getting his head around what the very young woman had said. He wasn't happy she had pulled him out of the room, but the way he always humored her was another point in his favor.

"Well, I don't want to talk in front of her, so I'm pulling you aside so we can discuss this," she said. "Do you see this? She's just a kid. If this is true, it's like… Oh my good God, Mark. Two kids? She was just a child, having a baby, two babies." She had to remind herself to keep her voice down, as she could feel the magnitude of what she was imagining as she stared at the license, the photo. The girl had shown up at Mark's door and shut down any chance of anything happening between them. Maybe that was why she was so rattled.

"Illegal, is that what you're going to say?" He inclined his head, those blue eyes flickering with passion and anger as if he were trying to piece together a puzzle.

"Yeah. I guess I'm looking for something that explains how illegal this is, but it isn't. Yet he killed her family? This is so bizarre. I just…"

He pulled those amazing strong arms over his chest. He wore a faded T-shirt and blue jeans that fit him too well, and his short red hair was unruly. She knew he was dangerous for her, but at the same time, his personality, the way he talked and listened, and even these complications that landed on his doorstep kept reeling her in again and again.

She knew deep down that Mark had never walked away from the kinds of problem a sane person would. Self-preservation didn't seem to be something he operated from, and maybe that was why she had to be around him. Good guys apparently did show up, though not as the picture-perfect image she had expected. He was like a drug for her.

"Look, right now there's a strange woman—"

"A girl, a teenager." She flicked the license she was still holding up to make her point.

"Fine, a teenager who looks like a woman and who showed up at my door with a story I haven't even heard the details of yet. I need to figure out whether a crime happened—and, if so, and this is a big if, can I even do something for her? Whether I'm disgusted or not is irrelevant, because unfortunately, this kind of shit happens in our country."

His hands were on his hips, and his gaze flickered with an anger she hadn't seen that often. "Yeah, I'm aware that all the advocacy groups fighting against child brides in shithole countries should start looking right under their noses at home. It's legal, as sick as it is."

He raised his brows, likely because she couldn't get her tongue to move, couldn't come up with one argument. Apparently, he knew this part of the law well, as did she.

"Do you need another minute in here?" he said. "Because I'd like to find out what the hell she wants and if there's something I can do. Unfortunately, on the child bride thing, there's zero, but on the murder thing, maybe."

He reached for the license and stood beside her, looking down at her, so close as he slid his hand to her hip and around. She could feel how pissed off he was, his passion, and damn, it only made her want him more.

"I can always tell, you know, when something treads on one of your no-go buttons," he said. His gaze lingered, and she wanted to run and hide, but his hand was still there, his arm across her. She had to fight the urge not to hold on to him.

"Fine," was all she could get out.

He pulled his hand away, and she was immediately furious, because even now, with a strange woman in his living room, she couldn't fight that pull toward him, and what bothered her more than anything was how well he could read her. Too well. She heard him pull open the door behind her, and when she turned, he was watching her.

"You coming?" he said, then dragged his gaze over to Lucky, who was still on the bed, tail wagging in expectation. "And you stay." He jabbed his finger at the dog.

Billy Jo followed him out to where Sunday was sitting. She was slender, dressed well.

He handed her license back to her. "Sorry about that…"

"You know, your walls are thin. Just FYI, I can hear everything you're saying, so if you're trying to save me any embarrassment or save face in trying to get rid of me, don't bother. It only makes this situation even more awkward. You think I don't know the statistics, the reality of how child marriage has been culturally accepted in the US? So many say the opposite, that it's child abuse, but it's not if a judge signs that piece of paper and weds you to a man who's old enough to be your father.

"You think I haven't looked for ways to get away from my husband? I even thought once, stupidly, that if the authorities only knew then I'd be pulled out, and he'd be in jail, and I'd be free of him. But that reality came crashing down when I called a lawyer one day when he was out only to hear that from 2000 to 2015, over two hundred thousand young girls in the US alone were wed legally to a man over eighteen. In too many states, I can't even enter a shelter, or divorce him, or leave him at all, because I'm a minor.

"I was screwed at thirteen, so you think I didn't look for any loophole to get away? That's why I sat outside your office for so long, knowing I couldn't walk in because I'd be seen, and you're damn right that I'm paranoid it will get back to him. I have a driver's license now, the only freedom I've had since I was forced to marry him, but I can't even run with my babies because there's nowhere to hide."

Billy Jo dragged her gaze over to Mark, who had pulled his cell phone from his pocket and was typing something in. He said nothing as she stepped over to him, and he held the screen out so she could see the title of the article he'd pulled up.

"As of July 2021, last month, six states have banned underage marriage with no exceptions. But not here," he said to Sunday.

She glanced at the first line of the article and angled her head. The way she looked at Mark, even Billy Jo could see she wasn't impressed, and all she could think was that for a sixteen-year-old, Sunday was unusually well composed.

"Sunday, I'm not sure what I can do," Mark said. "Does he hurt you? You said he killed your family. When, how? You're looking for help from me—to do what? To get away from him? To leave him? You said there are kids involved. Maybe you can do a wellness check, Billy Jo?" He looked over to her. She knew he was thinking over the options out loud.

Sunday cut in. "He's never laid a hand on the babies," she said.

Billy Jo flicked her gaze to Mark. "Let's play devil's advocate here. Say I did a wellness check. Then there'll be a report, and let's be real here. Sunday is only sixteen. The babies would be stuck in foster care. And that's not even addressing the issue of how I can suddenly get involved."

Mark stilled, saying nothing, his mouth open. He glanced up.

"You know, I can't be here much longer," Sunday said. "He'll wonder where I am since I said I was going to the store." She looked at her watch, and it wasn't lost on Billy Jo how calm she was, how this seemed like a game of cat and mouse.

"You said he killed your family," Mark said. "Start there and tell me what happened."

Her eyes were dark blue, her slender legs crossed, her hands linked over her knees. The diamond on her finger flickered. It was impressive. Nothing about her hinted at poverty. "Do you think I'm lying?"

Billy Jo narrowed her gaze. This young girl was playing a dangerous game. "Don't play coy! You showed up here, remember, at the door, looking for help, but all you've done since you walked in here was toss us a crumb. Is this a game for you? How about doing us all a favor and answering the question the chief asked you? Or are you lying about this, telling a story to jerk his chain and stir up trouble?"

Billy Jo felt Mark drag his gaze over to her, but there was something off about this girl. She couldn't help thinking this was a game, a lie, something to mess with Mark.

"I'm not lying about anything," Sunday said. "My husband, Ash Byrd, is a man people take their problems to. They tell him their problems, and he fixes them, and he's paid for it. My mom was a problem. When he showed up the first time and told her how it was going to be, he said they could resolve things the easy way or the hard way, but either way, it was going to happen.

"When my dad came home, she told him. I'd never seen her so scared. I don't know what she did, but she wouldn't stop even though I knew she was terrified. Next her tires were slashed, and her brakes were cut, and then the phone would ring and she'd scream at whoever was on the other end to leave her alone. She called the police once, but nothing happened.

"I asked my mom what that man wanted, what she'd done, and all she kept saying was that she was getting what she was owed. She worked in Hollywood for a producer. I heard her say once that the sharks in Chicago have nothing on Hollywood. She'd been fighting with actors, producers, managers.

"One day, I went to school. It was a Thursday in June. When I came home, Ash was sitting in my parents' living room alone. My parents were both gone. He told me that because my mom wouldn't do as she was told, and because she had gone to my dad and talked when she knew better, he'd had to take care of my dad as well. Then he said he had no choice but to make sure I couldn't be a problem. That was three years ago.

"Next, I was standing in a judge's chamber with him in a sunny California courthouse, thinking it was all a bad dream. But he said this was going to happen. So here I am, sixteen now, legally married to a man who fixes problems for the Hollywood elite. Now can you help me?"

Billy Jo couldn't pull her gaze from Sunday. When she finally did, looking over to Mark, she thought this really did sound like a young girl messing around with the new police chief.

Mark shook his head, making a sound of frustration under his breath as he dragged his gaze from her back to Sunday. "I'm confused. You said he killed your parents, yet you came home and he was in your house, your parents' house. Did you see him kill them? Where were their bodies? Was there a crime scene?"

Sunday lifted her purse over her shoulder and stood up, and Billy Jo couldn't believe she was seeing what seemed like arrogance. "No, there were no bodies, no crime scene. He's smarter than that, and it wasn't the first time he'd taken care of a problem. I'm married to the man, so I know that when he takes care of something, it goes away for good. No evidence will be found unless he wants it to. He has people working for him, from former cops to industry experts who understand the game."

Mark dragged his hand over his face, and she reached over and touched his arm. He looked right at her.

She just shook her head and said, "You should look into her parents, at least, see if any missing persons were reported."

And then he could call her out on her bullshit story, she thought, though she kept that part to herself. She didn't quite understand what it was about Sunday that rubbed her the wrong way.

Mark only groaned, then pulled his hand over his head, something he did when he didn't have an idea where to start. He didn't answer Billy Jo, just shook his head as he looked down at Sunday. "You probably already know what I'm going to say."

"Yeah, that you can't help me. No body, no crime, and there's no way it could be true. I can already tell she doesn't believe me," she snapped, gesturing to Billy Jo, which only angered her more. This girl was playing with fire, and it seemed she wasn't beyond taking a shot at her. "So thanks for nothing," she continued in a rather snarky tone, then started walking to the door.

"Wait." Mark lifted his hand.

Sunday's back was to him, her hand on the door, but she turned back and lifted her chin, all attitude. Billy Jo felt she was deliberately thumbing her nose at her. She knew she couldn't have explained this to anyone, this feeling that there was something so completely off about this girl.

"That wasn't what I was going to say," he said. "I'll look into it, see what I can find out, and if there is something, I'll see what I can do. But, one, if he killed your parents in California, it's out of my jurisdiction, and, two, as far as your marriage is concerned, until the laws are changed, there isn't a damn thing I can do about that. You live here, and he lives here too. I'll be in touch."

She pulled open the door. "No, please don't be in touch. I drove out here because he can't know I was talking to you," she said. Then she walked out the door.

Billy Jo took in Lucky, who was staring out at them from the bed, his tail wagging. Mark walked to the open door and pulled his cell phone from his pocket, and Billy Jo strode over to him and slid her hand to his back, leaning close to him as they watched the strange young woman walk to her fancy car, the kind

Billy Jo would never have tossed money toward. Mark lifted his phone, took a photo of it, and then looked down at her.

"You believe any of that story?" he said. From the way he was looking at her, she could see the edge of disbelief, and all she could do was shake her head. She'd thought for a moment that he'd believed it hook, line, and sinker.

"I don't know," she said. "A pretty young girl shows up at your door with a crazy story? If it's true, and I'm not saying it is, but if so, I think you'd better ask yourself just how much you want to stick your nose into this. Because if he is who she says, you don't have enough resources to investigate this, let alone go after someone like him. Problems you can't even imagine could very well land on your doorstep, and people could come after you. Or, worse, you could be made to disappear."

Chapter 4

Something about the visit from Sunday Byrd had completely cooled off anything happening between him and Billy Jo. Over a cold dinner, he hadn't gotten her to admit the parallels between her and Sunday, the many similarities. He'd never seen Billy Jo display the kind of open hostility she had to the young lady who'd knocked on his door. In the end, he'd slept alone with his dog at the foot of the bed.

Maybe that was one of the reasons he was feeling unsettled, off, and frustrated as he pulled up in front of the station in the early morning before anything else had opened and parked his Jeep beside Carmen's cruiser, seeing she was already there and the light was on inside. He didn't know where to begin in unraveling the tale of the girl who'd shown up at his door.

"Come on," he said to the dog, who jumped down and out the door. Mark's hair was still damp, and he held his go-mug of coffee and took a swallow as he stepped up on the sidewalk. He opened the door to find Carmen at her desk, on the phone, gesturing with a pen to his office, where a man he'd never seen before was sitting, having turned the chair to watch him. He had neat short dark hair and was casually dressed, not pulling his gaze from Mark.

"Bed, go," he said to Lucky, and the dog went right to his dog bed. Mark walked over to Carmen's desk as she hung up the phone. "Who is that?" he said.

She lifted her brows. "Don't know. He walked in and said you were expecting him. Said you'd know. I sent you a text a second ago before the phone rang."

Mark pulled his phone from his pocket and stared at a text sent five minutes earlier: *Some guy just showed up and is sitting in your office, waiting. Said you're expecting him.*

Carmen let her gaze linger on him, pissed off, as he glanced over to the man sitting there.

"You two finished gossiping out there?" the man said. "Come on in here, Mark. We need to have a talk."

Carmen's expression darkened. He didn't have a clue who the man was, but the way he spoke was unsettling. He heard the squeak of the chair and knew Carmen was on her feet behind him.

"You want me to get him out of here?" she said.

He shook his head. "No, I'll deal with this. Look, I sent you a text, a plate number. I want you to dig up anything you can on it, the registered owner, everything."

She was still standing there, her dark hair pulled back, looking at the man who was staring at them. He had to be forty, maybe, his hands linked over his belt, a thick gold ring with some insignia on his finger. He wasn't smiling.

Mark didn't look away as he said to Carmen, "I want to schedule a meeting later this morning with a couple of the possibilities to fill the deputy position and answer the phones here."

Then he started walking to his office, digging into each step. "You seem to know me, yet I'm at a loss. Have we met?" he said, standing just inside his office, staring down at the man, who stared right back at him, unflinching, cold. Mark couldn't remember ever looking into eyes so unfeeling before.

"Ash Byrd," the man said. "I can tell by your face that you already know why I'm here. Figured putting a face to the name would help. Join me. Come on in your office and sit down."

He had to fight the urge to look back at Carmen. He wanted to tell this guy to get the hell out of his office, but he remembered Billy Jo and her warning to him. He'd thought she was paranoid, but the memory now had him feeling like a fool. He was about to refuse and stand there, but something about this situation wasn't sitting right. With what he'd heard the night before about this man, he wondered what the hell had shown up in his community and on his island.

He glanced back once to Carmen, who was on her laptop, before walking around his desk, feeling each step. He heard his door close, and Ash turned to face Mark, who rested his coffee on his desk and sat and leaned back in his chair. He could feel his sidearm as he took in the man, wearing a long-sleeved burgundy Henley and dress pants he knew weren't from a bargain store. His face was clean shaven, with a scar on his chin.

"So what can I do for you—Ash Byrd, is it? You've walked right in here and made yourself at home. Do you forget I'm the chief of police?"

The man didn't smile as he pulled in a breath. "I know exactly who you are. You met my wife, Sunday, last night."

Mark was leaning back in his chair. He rocked a bit and didn't pull his gaze. How the hell did he know?

"Can see you don't want to answer," Ash said. "Not much goes on without my knowing."

Mark knew he made a face. "Now, why would you show up here and ask me that? What makes you think I've spoken with your wife?"

The man didn't flinch. Strength seemed to ooze from him. "You're new to the position here on the island, newly appointed, but good at what you do with the limited resources you have. The council here, though, doesn't really have your back, and they're looking for any reason to replace you with someone they want. After all, having you step in was only temporary, and much of this office really is in flux. You ever ask yourself how Tolly Shephard managed to keep his job as long as he did, running things the way he did? You ever ask who made sure he was left alone? I think you know what I'm talking about, given that bottom drawer of yours, which you haven't cleaned out."

Mark stilled, a knot in his stomach. He had to remind himself to breathe, picturing the file the chief had kept on Mary Jane and the other councillors, the dishonesty, the hands in the cookie jar, the kind of dirt that would serve as his insurance to keep the politicians in line and off his back.

"Sounds to me as if you're alluding to something," he said. "You help the chief out?"

He'd talk with Carmen, because how the hell did Ash have any idea what was in the bottom drawer unless he'd gone through it?

"No idea what you're talking about. Let's talk about the other situation, the tale you were told. You're a smart man, so let me help you out so you can stay smart and keep your job. Sunday is known for her tales. She's bored, and she finds you rather attractive, Chief, young and single as you are…"

Ash had big hands, he realized, as he gestured toward him, not pulling his gaze. Mark knew when someone was aware of what was going on around him without even looking. This guy was good, and as he recalled what Sunday had said, he felt his hand had already been tipped.

"Not sure what this is, but I'm not some wet-behind-the-ears rookie. Are you coming in here and threatening me? Because it sounds like you're trying to warn me off. Threatening an officer, I could arrest you for that."

"Who said anything about threatening you? We're just having a friendly conversation, is all."

Mark pulled in a breath, very aware of what he wasn't saying, being careful, giving nothing concrete. A smart man was sitting across from him. So that was how he was playing it. "Your wife, Sunday, an unusual name."

Ash's lips pulled to the sides in an odd smile. "Sure, young, smart, and troublesome…" He angled his head, teasing.

"How young is she, again?" Mark said. He knew he shouldn't, but this man already knew that he knew. How, he wasn't sure.

"You know, the greatest thing about this country is that the laws haven't caught up with me. There's nothing illegal about marrying a minor where we are right now."

"Thirteen is a kid, not a minor. It's child abuse."

Ash was shaking his head. "I know you're not an idiot there, Chief Mark Friessen. That snippy little social worker you spend time with knows what I'm talking about. Maybe you should have her fill you in on the legalese of a marriage document. She's my wife, and therefore there's no crime. Now, I'm coming here as a gentleman, all friendly, man to man. Because to hear that my wife is being entertained by another man, being shown interest by another man who just so happens to be the acting chief of police, well, I have to say I don't like that."

Mark just stared at him, realizing he was serious. He could feel the slippery slope he was treading, with this added dimension that was far from the truth. His job was everything, and the politics were never anything he had considered, but they had become more and more of what his job was. "Mr. Byrd, you come into my office, tossing out tales…"

"No, you're not listening to me, so I'm going to help you out so you understand. There's the easy way and there's the hard way, Chief Friessen. Doesn't matter which to me, but easier is better for everyone and for the community. It's never good for a police chief to be showing interest in a young girl. She's my wife, but to you, she's a minor. The community is still reeling from the sudden departure of Chief Shephard, a long-time resident who could be forgiven for far more than a new young chief no one knows much about other than his lack of respect for authority. Imagine being fired by a small county for taking bribes, corruption, and just being a bad cop in general. That's a bad way to go out."

The horror of what he'd said had Mark just staring at Ash as he stood up. He was of average height and weight, and he didn't know why he'd pictured someone with a lot of muscle. Ash pulled open the door and let his gaze linger on Mark again.

"You're creating a tale about me, and that's dangerous for you," Ash said, unflinching, confident in a way that was unsettling. "You think the truth is even relevant? You have a lot to learn. It was nice meeting you, Chief. Remember what I said."

Then he strode out to the door. Mark didn't get up. He could see Carmen already walking his way.

"What the hell was that about?" she said, gesturing.

Mark couldn't remember ever having been this unsettled. There was Billy Jo's warning again. He leaned forward, taking in the way Carmen was staring at him, wide eyed, freaked out. He pulled his hand over his face.

"Not sure, but I figure that was a warning," he said, then pushed back his chair and stood up to walk around his desk, past Carmen and over to the window. When he looked out, he couldn't see where Ash Byrd had gone. There were cars driving past, a few people here and there. Something about the warning made him feel a blindside coming.

"You ever hear of an Ash Byrd?" he said, turning back to Carmen.

She shrugged. "Is that who that was?"

He turned back to the window, aware she hadn't really answered. "He knows the chief," he said. When he turned back to Carmen, he wasn't sure he liked what he could see staring back at him. "He may have done some work for him."

She fisted her hands and nodded as she pulled them over her chest. "I presume we're not talking about the kind of work that would in any way be official."

Mark glanced back out the window. "No, nothing legal, legitimate, or above board here." He dragged his gaze away, around the empty and quiet station, to his dog, who was looking at him from the dog bed in the corner.

"I've never seen him before, but that doesn't mean anything," Carmen said. "The chief, you know, already had a way of doing things. But he also did business at the golf course, out where no one can hear you, where it's just two or three people and a golf game. A whisper here, a deal there… The chief played a lot of golf."

He took in Gail's empty desk, missing her more than he would admit. "Get me the details of that plate. It should come back as Ash Byrd's. Then I want you to find out everything about him, and I mean everything: who he knows, what he does, where he's from." Mark pulled his keys from his pocket and started to the door. "Come on, Lucky," he called to the dog.

"And where are you going?" Carmen said.

"To find out exactly what kind of problem is knocking at my door. You call me with anything," Mark said, then pulled open the door and let the dog out first, saying nothing else.

He walked down to his Jeep, unable to explain the odd feeling that someone was watching him. As he pulled open the door and let the dog in, he looked over his shoulder, but the problem was that he couldn't see anything or anyone out of place.

Chapter 5

Googling Sunday Byrd and her situation only to come up with nothing should have given Billy Jo some peace of mind. But something about the girl, her face, and her story bothered her in ways she couldn't have put into words. Worse, she was unsettled and furious because she'd seen the way Mark had looked at Sunday, and she knew he didn't see her the same way Billy Jo did.

She was perched on a stool at her small island with a coffee, her French press half full in front of her, Harley munching his kibble in a bowl on the floor, when she heard a vehicle. She was still in a T-shirt and pajama shorts, her hair a mess, but she heard footsteps on her stairs, so she closed up her laptop and slipped off the stool to walk barefoot over to the door just as there was a knock.

She flicked the deadbolt and pulled the door open, staring up to see vivid blue eyes, red hair, and brooding lips. She remembered too well what those felt like pressed to hers, and she let her gaze linger. He took in her bare legs, her pajamas, and she could see he had something on his mind.

"I need to talk to you," he said.

She stepped back, and he walked right in, wearing blue jeans, a jean jacket, and cowboy boots, with the greatest ass she'd ever seen. There was something about Mark. Being around him was the easiest and the hardest thing at the same time. She closed the door and swept back her shoulder-length hair, feeling the tangles. Mark was already in her kitchen, making himself at home, pulling out a mug from the cupboard as she strode back over to the island and slid back onto the stool. He lifted the French press and poured himself a coffee, and she waited, seeing the moodiness and how off he was.

"I hope this isn't where you're going to start in on me again," she said, and he was still holding the French press. He filled her mug to the top, emptying what was left. His lips were tight, and he clearly didn't want to talk.

"What was it you said, that I'm like Sunday Byrd?" she said. He put the empty French press into the sink without responding. "You know, Mark, you have a blind spot when it comes to attractive women, and Sunday, though sixteen, is that and then some. You have any idea what it's like to sit there and watch you just accept everything she said? You ever heard of a woman who knows how to spin it, to dial up the drama, to mess with you? Pretty sure that tattoo on your arm should be enough of a reminder of how nice, gorgeous girls can flash you a smile and tell you a story while lying through their teeth."

"Do you want me to say I'm sorry?" He rested both hands on the island, staring right at her. "I will if that will help, but just the same, Billy Jo, I'm not going to start lying to you now. You want me to tell you what you want to hear, or do you want me to tell you the truth? I thought this thing here, with us, starts with no bullshit." He gestured at her.

She could feel this going sideways again. "Don't be an asshole, Mark, or toss out cruel comparisons between me and Sunday, because there are no similarities between us, what I went through, and her showing up at your door."

"Yeah, but one minute you want me to check into it, and the next you're calling her a liar."

She fisted her hands, resting them on the island, wondering when he'd become so good at tossing attitude right back at her. "I never called her a liar, so you're putting words in my mouth, but you think a young girl like that isn't stretching the truth? Look at her. The only reason we knew she was young was because of the ID she offered rather easily. Then there was the game of sitting outside the station, not wanting to come in because she's afraid of it getting back to her husband. I have to wonder, is it even true? The cloak and dagger and drama are very indicative of a story from someone so young, and you fell for it. I could see how adept she was at reeling you in. You're telling me you don't find her attractive in the least?"

She'd never seen him look at her quite the way he was, with anger and fury flickering in those blue eyes.

"She's a fucking kid," he said. "Seriously, don't turn me into a creep eyeing up a young girl. She knocked on the door looking for help, is all. I'm the chief of police here. You're damn right I'm going to give any woman looking for help the benefit of the doubt. I'm surprised as all hell with you, Billy Jo. You're so quick to toss out her story and paint her as a liar. I would've thought out of anyone, you'd have been in her corner, advocating, fighting. You know, you may not want to admit it, but she hit a nerve in you. I saw it last night. Whether it's her story, her situation, or the girl herself, I could see it in the way you walked out on me. Even right now, you're ready to go another round."

She wondered if that was the reason he appeared so pissed. "You swallowed everything she said as if it were gospel. With her showing up at your door with that story, maybe some of it's true, but maybe the whole thing is absolute bullshit. I could see the way you looked at her. She's attractive, young. You were ready to bend over backwards for her, letting her lead you around…"

"Don't you fucking dare, not from you too." He slammed his mug down, cutting her off, and the coffee sloshed over the side. The cat jumped, and Billy Jo stared back at the flicker of fire in his eyes. She realized what he'd said.

"What do you mean, not from me too?"

His mouth was tight as he reached for the roll of

paper towel, ripped off a sheet, and wiped up the spilled coffee. "You know, Billy Jo, suggesting I could seriously be eyeing up that girl is pretty low, even for you. She's a kid. You think I don't know you're more scared of yourself and this bullshit relationship, this dancing around that you're doing with me? You'd rather paint me as a dirty dog because then you could say, 'Look, I was right, see?'"

She flicked her gaze to her coffee, feeling the slap and the embarrassment, then lifted her hands. "I'm sorry. I know you wouldn't cross the line. But are you honestly telling me you didn't find her attractive in the least bit?"

He angled his head and narrowed his gaze, then let out a rude sound under his breath. "You don't get it. That suggestion is the kind of thing that could ruin my life, my career. It's not even funny, Billy Jo, and I can't believe you of anyone would accuse me. Why would you even think so little of me? In all the time we've spent together, are you telling me you really believe I would go around with another woman behind your back? You really believe I could do that?" He could really be loud when he was pissed off—no, furious.

For a moment, she felt herself stumbling, trying to explain how she had to fight every day the doubts that plagued her. "No… I'm sorry. I didn't mean it like that."

"Really, then how did you mean it?"

She pulled in one breath and then another. "Look at me and look at you."

He narrowed his gaze and made another rude sound as if he didn't get it. "And what exactly are you trying to get at? Is this about me being a cop and you a social worker or what? Because you've lost me."

She just stared and could feel her jaw slacken, wondering how he didn't see that she wasn't a supermodel, the typical woman he was drawn to, attractive, gorgeous, with curves. "I don't want to fight with you, Mark. What did you mean when you said not from me too? You didn't answer me."

He really did appear off. "I walked into the station this morning to find a man I'd never seen before sitting in my office, waiting to give me a message. He walked right past Carmen, telling her I was expecting him." He pulled his hand over the back of his neck, and his jean jacket pulled back to reveal his firearm, his badge.

She knew she was pushing him away, and she didn't want to. She wondered why she couldn't just be happy. "Who was waiting for you, Mark?"

He looked right at her across the distance she'd created. "It seems Ash Byrd knew Sunday paid me a visit last night. He was there, sitting in my office, making himself at home, waiting to warn me off. Yeah, she's married to him, so she's not lying about that, Billy Jo. I think he knows the chief and did some work for him, too."

She wondered what kind of odd look was on her face. "What kind of work?"

He lifted his mug and downed his coffee, then walked over to the sink and rinsed it out before setting it there. She wanted to yell at him to say something, as she could feel her heart pounding. She'd never seen him this rattled.

"Remember the files the chief had to keep the council in line, the dirt on each of them in the bottom of my desk? Seems Ash may have been the one to collect it for him."

She didn't lean forward but realized he was serious. "For real?"

He shrugged. "It's why I'm here. I plan to go see the chief and ask him outright who this guy is, but whoever he is, I know he's the kind of guy I wouldn't want to meet in a dark alley alone. You know he even went so far as to discredit Sunday? You know, saying she's a flirt, a storyteller, and it wouldn't look good if people suddenly learned the chief of police on this island is messing around with someone's sixteen-year-old wife."

She knew her jaw slackened, and she stared in horror, now recognizing the look on his face. He was cornered, upset, scared. "He seriously said that to you, accusing you of messing around with her? So he's planning on tossing out a story about you to get you to back off. You told him what she said?"

Mark was looking away, leaning against the sink. When he dragged his gaze back to her, it wasn't filled with the same caring she'd become used to. Why did she insist on pushing him away?

"No, I told her last night I wouldn't tell her husband, and my word means something, Billy Jo. I haven't had a chance to look into her story. I gave the plate number to Carmen and asked her to dig up anything she could on Ash Byrd. But he knew enough. Whether she went home and told him…" He gestured vaguely. "Nevertheless, he's right about one thing. If a story got out about me showing interest in a young girl, I'd be run off the island, and it wouldn't matter what I have on the council. My job would be gone. That's the kind of thing I couldn't run from. It would follow me. As you've already pointed out, Billy Jo, with my history with women, it really wouldn't be too much of a leap, now, would it?"

She could hear the nastiness in his voice, and maybe she deserved that slap. She wanted to say people wouldn't believe it, but she knew that wasn't true. "I'm sorry, Mark. What are you going to do?"

He sighed. "I don't know. Go see the chief, have a word with him about Ash Byrd, find out who he is, what he does for people, exactly, and everything about Sunday."

Then he started walking out of the kitchen right past her. No hug, no kiss, no nothing.

"Mark," she called out to him.

He stopped halfway to the door and glanced back to her.

"I don't really believe you'd do that," she said. "It's just my own insecurity."

He nodded. "I know, but there is a point, Billy Jo, where you can go too far, push too hard, lashing out to slap me down and push me away. I wouldn't do that to you, not ever," he said.

Then he kept walking out the door, and she shut

her eyes, feeling his words and knowing how right he was. As Mark went down the stairs, Lucky barked from where he'd evidently been left in the Jeep.

Billy Jo realized she needed to get her head right, or this thing with Mark would never go anywhere. Because he was right: She was pushing him out of her life because he knew too many of her dark and dirty secrets, and he could read her way too well, and that was the one thing that absolutely terrified her.

Chapter 6

"Damn, damn, damn, why?" Billy Jo said as she flicked her gaze to her rear-view mirror, taking in her eyes, dull blue, her straight mousy brown hair, and the freckles she'd always hated. She felt like absolute shit, the knot tightening in her stomach as she realized she'd gone from the girl who'd caught Mark's eye to the girl who was driving a knife into his heart. "There's something seriously wrong with you. Get it together."

She was driving down an island road, down a driveway shrouded with trees, seeing Gail's white truck and Mark's Jeep. Her heart thudded because she suddenly felt awkward and stalkerish as she pulled in and stopped behind it.

"You just can't help yourself, can you, going from one stupid thing to the next? You shouldn't be here, Billy Jo." She looked again at her reflection, trying to figure out how to explain her showing up there without sounding like a nutcase. Then the front door opened, and she knew it was too late as she took in Gail standing there, staring at her.

She turned off the car and let out a sigh as she pulled open the door and stepped out. As she closed it, Gail didn't pull her gaze, unsmiling, wearing blue jeans. Lucky was racing out the front door toward her.

"Hey there, good boy," she said. "Missed you this morning." She rubbed the dog's side and knew she was stalling, so she forced herself to look up to Gail and did something she'd never done before: She pasted on a smile.

"Oh good God, what's wrong?" Gail said, alarm flashing across her face. It had the knot in Billy Jo's stomach twisting more, and she nearly stumbled.

"Nothing is wrong. Why would you ask that?" Billy Jo clutched her keys and watched as Lucky walked right back into the house past Gail, making himself completely at home. Billy Jo took in the woman she'd always have a soft spot for.

"Your face," Gail said. "One thing I like about you is that as long as I've known you, you've never pretended to be something you're not. Some girls can pull off that fake smile, but you're not one of them. So what is it?"

She stopped in front of Gail, hearing voices inside, the chief and Mark. She had realized while driving in that she didn't have a reason to explain this madness. "Mark is here?"

Gail only lifted a brow.

Billy Jo let out a sigh. "Fine. I screwed up big time

and said something I wish I hadn't, and I feel like an absolute asshole…"

Gail shook her head and rolled her eyes, stepping back and gesturing inside. "You mean with Mark? So you're here to apologize, make it right. Boy, this I have to see," Gail said, and Billy Jo nodded as she stepped inside. Gail took her in, letting her gaze linger and then drop lower. "You look rather fresh."

She angled her head and took in the teasing smile that appeared on Gail's face. "Fresh, what the hell does that mean?" She felt her shoulders pulling forward, feeling a wave of unease about the light green V-cut blouse that made her feel more like a girl than she was comfortable with.

"You can really fill out a pair of blue jeans nicely. Seems you've been hiding all that hotness under boxy and plain clothes. There's nothing boxy and plain with how you look now. Boy, you really are sunk, aren't you? Well, come on in…" Gail started walking.

Billy Jo found herself looking back at the closed door, wondering whether it was too late to walk back out, climb in her car, and drive away. After all, how was she going to explain the craziness of her just showing up there?

As she followed Gail into the family room, which overlooked the open-concept kitchen, she took in the box of the chief's photos and memorabilia. Mark was staring at her with an odd expression, his gaze narrowed, whereas the old chief looked at her the same way he always had. Evidently, his fondness for her hadn't grown.

"Look who I found at the door," Gail said.

Billy Jo's heart thudded, and she took in the deep green loveseat Gail stood in front of, glancing back to her. Mark and the chief were each in an easy chair, the stone fireplace between them, and everyone was staring at her, waiting for her to say something, anything, about why she was there.

"Sorry I'm late," she said, looking right at Mark. All he did was lift a brow. She could feel the chief watching her, and she thought Gail was laughing at her. "Can I talk to you a second?" she continued without moving or pulling her gaze.

As Mark stood up and took a step over to her, Gail walked around him to the old chief and said, "Tolly, I need your help."

She gestured, and the chief pushed himself out of the chair. She had expected him to at least ask what she wanted or say no, but to his credit, he said none of that, instead following her down the hall obediently. That left her with Mark standing right in front of her, his jean jacket still on. Her eyes went right to that magnificent chest, and she pulled in a breath and lifted her gaze to those unsmiling vivid blue eyes.

"What are you doing here?" he said.

"I don't like how you left, and I wanted to say I'm sorry, because you're right."

He didn't blink or make a face. Something about the way he could hold her gaze was really unnerving. "You showed up at the chief's, where I'm trying to find out about Ash Bryd, to say you're sorry, seriously?"

Having him point out to her how ridiculous this seemed didn't help the awkwardness she was feeling.

"I know this is crazy, and I realized as soon as I pulled up here that it was ridiculous, but then Gail opened the door, and it was too late to drive away. So here I am, feeling stalkerish, trying to save face. I feel way out of my depth, and I'm so very sorry for what I said. I can't believe I accused you of being interested in Sunday Byrd. I know you're not that kind of creep. It was just my—"

"Issues, insecurity," Mark cut in, and Billy Jo found herself gritting her teeth because it felt as if he were shoving it in her face. "Are you still going to deny this is personal for you?"

At least he hadn't compared her to Sunday again. She resisted the urge to roll her shoulders, feeling the tightness and the pinching, fighting her first instinct to run out and walk away, pulling herself kicking and screaming from her comfort zone. This was so damn hard.

"I still don't believe she's telling the truth, not about everything," she said. "You find out about Ash Byrd yet from the chief?"

From the way he nodded, she wondered whether he was agreeing with her or conceding and not pushing her to admit that maybe he was right. There was too much about Sunday that she didn't like, and those qualities were the same ones she had hidden inside herself.

"Just got here. Didn't have a chance to get into anything too much," he said.

Billy Jo made herself reach over and press her hand to his arm. He angled his head, and his expression softened, but he didn't make a move even though he'd been the one in their relationship to make every single move to that point, giving a touch, a kiss, some support.

And she'd fought him every step of the way.

"You two kiss and make up yet?" Gail called out.

Damn, was this awkward. Mark gave a soft chuckle under his breath. He must have figured out how terrified Billy Jo was of herself. He slid his hand over her shoulder and stepped up close beside her. His touch said everything.

"Yeah, we're fine, Gail. You can come on back in now," he called out.

Billy Jo shut her eyes for a second, feeling mortified, and maybe Mark understood, as he squeezed her shoulder again. Meanwhile, the dog trotted in with what looked like a rawhide bone in his mouth, lay down in the middle of the family room, and started chewing. Yeah, Gail and Tolly really did have a soft spot for Lucky.

When they followed the dog in, Mark gestured to the loveseat and looked right at Billy Jo.

"So you didn't ask about Sunday, either?" she said in a low voice to him. "I searched the internet and didn't find anything on either of them."

He only shrugged as he sat right beside her, so close, and glanced over to her. "I wasn't here long enough to ask anything before you got here."

The chief sat back down in the same easy chair,

and Gail took the other. "I know this isn't a social call, Mark," he said. "You said you needed to talk to me about a potential problem. I'm all ears."

She looked at Mark, who was leaning forward, his forearms resting on his knees. She reached over and pressed her hand to Mark's arm again, and of course he looked her way. "Last night there was a knock on Mark's door," she said. "It was a young woman by the name of Sunday Byrd with quite a story. Sixteen yet married for three years already, looking for help. She said her husband, Ash, killed her family, and she was forced to marry him. She has two children already. This morning, Ash greeted Mark in his office. He was sitting and waiting for him, knowing his wife had been over last night."

Mark was looking right at her, and she rubbed his arm before pulling her hand away and flicking her gaze to Tolly, who looked over to Gail. Whatever passed between them, she realized they already knew something.

"You say he was waiting for you when you went in," the chief said.

Mark dragged his gaze back over to him. "He'd walked in before I got there, told Carmen I was expecting him, made himself at home. But what really bothers me is how well he knew your office. He talked about the file in the bottom drawer, the information on the council, what you left for me. That was after he warned me away from his wife. How he knew she was at my place, I have no idea, considering I promised her I wouldn't say anything. Maybe she told him. So I have to wonder, Chief, did you have him dig up that dirt for you? Because our conversation had me wondering how well he knows you and you him. So who is he, and do I have something to worry about?"

Mark gestured to the chief, waiting, as an unspoken conversation seemed to pass between Gail and Tolly.

"Are you going to tell him?" Gail said in a way that made Billy Jo suspect she might not like what she was about to hear.

"He showed up to warn you off, did he?" the chief said, then shook his head, and the knot in Billy Jo's stomach only tightened further. Mark wasn't looking her way, and she found herself sliding closer to him.

"You evidently know him," Mark said.

The chief made a face. "Yeah, I know Ash. So Sunday showed up at your place. My advice, Mark? You need to forget she was ever there, and if she shows up again, you send her on her way. Yeah, Ash takes care of problems for those who can afford it, if you know what I mean. I didn't pay him, if that's what you're asking, but he showed up one day because the council was politicizing and jerking my chain to get me to follow their orders. He knew, everyone knew. I knew who he was, as you learn quickly who's who on this island, those who come and go. He had found out everything about who was calling the shots in the council, with everyone else just following along. So, after we had a conversation, he provided that information to me. He even had a word with the famous three, Mary Jane Trundell, Herb

Walker, and Hal Green, to let them know messing with me would be their downfall."

Even Billy Jo knew what he meant by that, considering how much her dad had shared with her, growing up, about how things worked in politics. But it seemed this was different.

"So it was a gift to keep you quiet, out of his business. You knew about his child bride?" Billy Jo cut in. When Mark turned his head back to her, she wondered whether he was expecting her to be quiet. If so, that wasn't going to happen.

"Ash Bryd is from California," the chief said. "He made his money there and has an office in Hollywood, with a part-time home here on the island. Agents, managers, big producers, and the Hollywood elite hire him when stars get themselves in trouble, and he fixes the problem. He's probably the best around. So if he showed up and warned you off, you need to listen. You don't mess with Ash Byrd." He spoke so matter of factly, dragging his gaze over to Billy Jo, "And let's be clear on something. Sunday Byrd is his wife. She may be underage, but what he did is completely legal. In California, there is no minimum age to marry. So there's no crime there. You have a problem with any of that, write your congressman and change the law."

Billy Jo felt the slap. She wasn't sure what to make of the way Gail was watching Tolly.

"So you're telling me that if I don't let it go, he'll make good on his word?" Mark said. "He threatened to see to it that word gets out that I'm hooking up with his child bride. Even though he's married to her, I'd suddenly be seen in this community as a predator of young girls. I'd be run off the island, and the council would have all the ammunition they needed to fire me."

Maybe hearing Mark say it now was what made Billy Jo realize how bad this was. He was the one guy who didn't walk away when someone was in trouble. It went against everything he was.

"Word of advice, Mark. In this one, you're going to have to park your integrity. I know it goes against who you are, but if Ash Byrd warned you off, that was the gentleman in him giving you a courtesy, a heads-up that you crossed a line. Ther's no second chance. Let's be clear on what will happen. You will wake up one morning with a shitstorm of allegations against you, likely learning first about it in the news—sexual impropriety, maybe assault, or maybe you just have a thing for young girls. There will be no mention whatsoever of Ash Byrd or his marriage.

"You'll be in front of the firing squad, and you won't be able to talk your way out of it. It will be dirty, ugly, and you won't have a leg to stand on with the council, because the Feds will likely be investigating you. You'll find yourself facing charges, a criminal indictment, and whether you fight it or not will be irrelevant, because you'll never win against the federal government. And that's the best-case scenario, because you just might not survive going up against Ash Byrd.

"You know, Mark, there's a saying. If you want to

make a lot of money, go to Wall Street. If you want to spend a lot of time with gorgeous women, go into the modeling business. If you want to have power over people's lives, go to Washington. If you want all three, money, sex, and power, go to Hollywood. Because in Hollywood, you can access things you can't anywhere else.

"That's who Ash Byrd is. He's the power behind the scenes, the one who fixes the problems of the Hollywood elite, and that includes the judges, the attorney general, the elected representatives in California. I'm sure you're already figuring out that half this island is owned by the California who's who." Tolly was leaning forward, and Gail was now standing.

Billy Jo knew that was their cue. Mark looked back to her, and she patted his arm again and stood up when he did.

"Well, thanks for coming, you two," Gail said. "I'll have you both over for dinner soon."

It wasn't lost on Billy Jo that she was shutting down the conversation about the Byrd family. Mark called Lucky, who still had the rawhide bone in his mouth, and followed the chief to the door. Billy Jo was following him, unable to make out what Mark was saying to the chief, when she felt a hand on her arm, pulling her back. She glanced up to Gail.

"You think she's lying, don't you?" Gail said in a low voice so Mark and Tolly couldn't hear.

"About some of it, I do, and maybe more."

Gail looked to the door and then back to her.

"You keep Mark away from her," she said, her voice just above a whisper. "Because Ash will break him. He's no joke. He's good at what he does, which is why he's the one the Hollywood elite call when they find themselves on the front page, with trouble dogging them. As far as Sunday, be careful with her. She may be just a kid, but she's smart as all hell. My guess is she wants something. Ash is dangerous, but Sunday has been with him long enough that she knows how to play. And for both your sakes, don't talk about this with anyone."

Billy Jo knew Mark was waiting. She realized Gail knew a lot more than she was saying. She'd never seen her so on edge before. "And her story, you think it's true?"

Gail dropped her hand from Billy Jo's arm and stepped back. "We'll do a barbecue, catch up," she said loud enough that Mark could hear. Then she was walking to the door, and Billy Jo realized that was her cue to leave. She wasn't getting anything else.

As she walked out the door with Mark, the dog running around the Jeep, she heard the front door close behind them, and Mark reached for her arm and said, "So what was that?"

She took in his warm hand and how close he was standing. "I don't know, Mark. A warning, maybe. I have a bad feeling here."

He didn't say anything at first, and she took in his expression, the way he glanced past her, thinking. She was very aware of his moods, and that scared her.

"Yeah, fuck," he said, "but here we are."

She nodded. "I hate to say this, Mark, but I wish Sunday had never knocked on your door."

He squinted in the sun and then let his gaze settle on her. "Wishing isn't going to fix this or make it go away. You off to work?"

Right. Her appointments, her schedule, the kids she needed to check in on.

She nodded and said, "Do me a favor."

He was still looking at her. "Am I going to want to hear this?"

She touched him again, this time pressing her hand to the flat of his chest. Damn, she'd never touched him this much before. His gaze dropped to her hand. "Don't do anything today about Sunday," she said.

He pressed his hand over hers and squeezed, pulling it away but not letting go as he said, "You know I can't do that." He leaned in and hesitated only a second before pressing a kiss to her lips and pulling back. "I'll call you later."

Then he pulled open his Jeep and let the dog in, and Billy Jo wished that Mark, just this one time, would not be the hero.

Chapter 7

For the second time that day, Mark pulled in and parked in front of the island station-house. He found himself really looking around, taking in the hotel and restaurant across the road, the cars on the street, and the stores. The island was now into its morning routine. Lucky jumped out, having dropped the rawhide bone on the backseat, and was quickly at the door to the office.

Nothing about his stopover at the chief's had given him the answers he wanted to hear. Instead, it had left him with a heaviness settling over him.

He turned the knob and opened the door to see Carmen and two new faces, and he took a second to wonder what the hell was coming at him now.

"Oh, hi, Chief," Carmen said as she jumped up from her chair.

He took in a tall, lanky young man with light hair and freckles, wearing blue jeans that hung on his too-thin frame, and a woman with light blond hair pulled back and pinned up, wearing what looked like a brown deputy shirt. She flashed him a bright smile.

"Just sit down, both of you," Carmen said quite sharply to the two, and they sat in the chairs in front of her desk.

As Mark closed the door, Carmen hurried over to him, her expression too weird for him to try to decipher.

"What's going on?" he said, gesturing with his keys in his hand, letting his gaze linger on the guy and girl, who were both staring at him with smiles pasted on their faces. He settled his hands on his waist and just looked down at them, then gave his head a shake and kept walking into his office. He heard Carmen say something to them in a low voice as he walked around his desk and dropped his keys, and the dog followed him in. He sat down in his chair, looking out into his precinct.

"You want to explain who that is out there?" he said to Carmen, whom he couldn't remember ever looking so awkward. She reached for the door and closed it, but from the glassed-in office, he could see everything.

"They're the new deputy and dispatcher," she said, and he was pretty sure she winced.

He shot her a look and flicked his gaze back out to take in the two sitting there, looking his way. They lifted their hands and waved at him.

"Excuse me? Who sent them? Because I'm pretty sure I didn't call anyone to come in yet and interview, let alone decide on someone to fill the vacancies."

"They showed up an hour ago with Hal Green. He said the council has already hired them, and they have signed contracts."

Mark leaned back hard in his chair, hearing the squeak, and linked both his hands over his belt as he listened to Carmen. Someone was jerking his chain from behind the scenes, and he didn't like that feeling at all.

"You're telling me Hal Green walked in here while I was gone and said those two sitting at your desk now work here?"

Carmen glanced over her shoulder and then back to him and nodded. "Correct. He said something along the lines of your being too busy, and since they already sent over the resumes of their picks, they just figured it would be easier to take it off your plate and finalize it. They have contracts and are apparently starting right now."

Unbelievable. It seemed nothing about today would be easy or smooth. He nodded. "Well, that's just fucking great. Seems I'm getting my hands tied from every direction," he said, though he knew Carmen didn't understand. He gestured to her. "You find out anything on Ash Byrd and that plate number I gave you?"

Carmen didn't often show she was rattled, but he could see she was a little thrown. "Plate you gave me is registered to him. He owns a house up on Sanders, top of the hill, twenty-five acres. Gated, too. What I could find on him is that he's some type of consultant, with an office in Hollywood and a staff of five but no website. That's it. No social media, nothing online, and no company reviews, so that tells me…"

"He works for the who's who, and having a public profile works against him," Mark cut in, rocking a bit in his chair. Lucky was sitting now, looking up to him and panting.

"So what do you want me to do?" Carmen said. "You want to send those two packing? I have to say, Chief, we need the help now. There's the phones, and no one is doing rounds because I'm here taking care of this place, which Gail always did. You know Gail's shoes are going to be hard to fill. She had her finger on the pulse of this community, and she knew how this office and everything runs."

"Get one of them to fill Lucky's bowl with water and get him some kibble. Then send me Byrd's address." He stood up and grabbed his keys from his desk, taking in his dog and a wide-eyed Carmen, who gestured to him.

"So you want me to put them to work?" she said.

He dragged his gaze to the two, who were now talking. The man looked over to him and tapped the woman, who also looked his way. "Nope," Mark said. "Get one of them on dog duty, but I'm going to have a word with them both after I pay the council a visit, because they do not get to hire my people."

Then there was Ash Byrd. Mark didn't have a clue how he was going to handle that. Add in Billy Jo, who confused the hell out of him, and today was shaping into the kind of tough day where everything that could go wrong would.

"Word of advice, Mark?" Carmen pressed her hand to his desk, and in that suddenly personal moment, he realized another warning was coming.

"Why not? Seems to be a day of advice," he said. He could see her confusion in the way her brows knit, but at least she didn't ask.

"I've been working here a long time," she said. "You may not have liked Chief Shephard's way of doing things, but he handled the council so things worked for him, and most times they did. As the chief explained to me not long after I started, when he was training me, it took him a while to figure out the way of things. He said they're like snakes. You walk out thinking you've agreed to do things one way, and before you're even back in your office, you find a knife in your back. They'll suggest something and you'll say no, and you'll think that's the end of it, yet they'll do it anyway. Or they'll cut your legs right out from under you and force your hand. They operate totally differently than we do, using some obscure playbook. But Chief Shephard managed for the most part to keep the council hands off when it came to running this department, and that included their not influencing investigations or telling him how he was to interpret the law. Do you understand what I'm saying? He never once went in there and had a showdown, which I can see you very much want to do. Trust me when I say it will backfire on you. Think first. Be smart."

He knew what she was saying, but he wasn't about to take this lying down. "Thanks, Carmen. I do appreciate the shared wisdom, but I'm well aware of what I'm dealing with, and I'm not going to be made a fool of."

Carmen pulled open the door, and Mark gestured to the dog, who ran out ahead of both of them. He followed her out of his office and took in the two council recruits, who were standing now, their expressions eager.

"You do exactly what she says and touch nothing," was all Mark said to them on his way out. "And someone get my dog some water and kibble!"

Then he pulled open the door and stepped out, shutting his eyes for a second, because it seemed policing this island had become the last job he was doing.

HE COULD HAVE WALKED to the council office because it was only a block away, but instead he drove. As he parked at midday in front of the two-story white-washed building with an American flag waving in front, a town worker was weeding the flower garden, and the automatic sprinkler was running. The lawn was well manicured, so he could see taxpayer money was being well used.

He shook his head as he stepped out of his Jeep. The day was warm already as he strode up to the commercial glass front door, his cowboy boots scraping the stone steps. He pulled off his sunglasses and stepped inside, where he took in the bright, flirty smile of the council assistant as she greeted him.

"Chief Friessen, how are you today?"

What was her name again, Jeanette, Jane, Julie? He leaned on the counter, taking in her round face, shoulder-length dark hair, and sleeveless silky blue shirt. She was attractive, in her early twenties, but he wasn't interested in the least.

"Hal Green in?" he said, but he heard voices down the hall before she could say anything, and he leaned back to spot Hal and Mary Jane herself coming out of a boardroom. "Never mind. There they are…" he said, then patted the counter and started walking down the hall. It was Mary Jane who saw him first.

"Mark, what a surprise. Didn't know we had a meeting scheduled," she said. Mary Jane was neat and tidy, attractive in a conservative way, her makeup flawless and her smile perfect. Hal, though, was balding and of average height, and his smile reminded Mark of a used car salesman.

"We don't have a meeting," he said. "I came to have a word with Hal, but it's even better that you're here so I have to say this only once."

Mary Jane gave a sharp shake of her head. "Mark, I don't have time today. I have another meeting in ten minutes."

"It won't take that long," he said, sensing she was trying to blow him off. He gestured to the office in front of him with her name on the door. "Shall we?"

Mary Jane's unsmiling expression held something

he wasn't familiar with, and it gave him that off feeling. "Five minutes only, Mark," she stressed as she strode into her office.

Mark waited for Hal to walk in as well, but the man didn't move. Instead, he said, "No, after you, Mark."

So the power play had begun. Mark walked in ahead of Hal and glanced back to him as he closed the door. Mary Jane was standing behind her desk, wearing a silky black shirt with ruffles and a pencil skirt. She was slim, and he knew her pumps weren't overly high.

"So what can I do for you, Mark?" she said, sounding quite short, all business.

"You can both explain to me why Hal walked into my precinct today with two newbies and told my detective they're the new recruits. You do not have jurisdiction over hiring. Who I hire is my call."

"I completely understand," Hal said, "and if I was in your position, I'd likely feel the same way. But here's the thing, Mark. We sent you the resumes of our picks, who we feel would work best for this community…"

"Last night. You sent over your picks last night," Mark said, cutting off Hal, whose phony plastic smile he wanted to wipe off his face. "Are you telling me that between last night and today, you decided to just go ahead and hire them? Well, you're going to have to un-hire them and explain to them why they don't have the job."

Mary Jane was no longer even pretending to

smile. No, looking back at him was a woman who knew how to run things her way. "We can't do that, Mark. They're under contract with the council, on payroll, so you're just going to have to make it work. Train them and get them to work. The detective is on a one-year contract, and the dispatcher is on a nine-month—"

"Detective? I have a detective, Carmen. We've been through this already. The only job openings are for a deputy and dispatcher to fill Gail's position." He was very direct and unusually calm.

Mary Jane let out a heavy sigh and looked over to Hal, who was still standing by the door, his arms crossed, leaning against it. Mark saw an arrogance in him that he'd never liked.

"We, the council, never approved Carmen's promotion," Hal said, "and in case you may have forgotten, we pay her salary and yours. As far as the council is concerned, she was only filling in until someone with the necessary qualifications could be contracted. We've taken care of that for you. Oh, and another thing, Chief." Hal uncrossed his arms and rested his hand on the doorknob, ready to pull it open.

Mark said nothing, pulling in one breath and then another.

"I understand there may have been a discrepancy in the handling of the budget for the island homeless," Hal continued, "but I believe that's been rectified. Seems our dear Jennifer out front isn't quite as efficient with the bookkeeping as she let on. But we wouldn't want her to lose her job over it. Nor would we want something of this seriousness to get out, because it would be a black mark that would forever trail her. It could possibly even end with her being charged with a misdemeanor. I mean, that's not fair, but if you insist on pushing…" He pulled open the door, and his smile widened.

Mark just stared in horror, hating the man and how he was suddenly two steps ahead of him. When he looked back at Mary Jane, she wore a hard expression as she linked her fingers and stared at him unapologetically. She lifted her wrist, glancing to her watch. Yeah, this was no surprise to her.

"Wow, absolutely fucking amazing, both of you," was all he got out before Mary Jane said, "Okay, now we're done. I have a meeting. Mark, you can show yourself out."

And that was that.

Hal was now outside the office, still smiling, standing in the hall. Mark only shook his head, because there was that feeling again of having the rug yanked out from under him.

"Close the door behind you, please," Mary Jane said as she sat in her black high-back executive chair, reaching for the phone.

Mark pulled the door closed behind him, and that left Hal and him in the hallway. "You think you're smarter than me," he said, unable to help himself.

Hal's expression was smug. "Be careful, Detective. That sounds like a threat."

Mark took a step toward him, putting all his aggression into each step, his hands fisted, and Hal jumped back, maybe because he wasn't as stupid as he'd first thought. "You be careful there, Councillor. You may have found yourself a scapegoat, but there's one thing I know about snakes like you. If you had your hand stuck in one thing, there will be another, and now I'll be waiting. You may be slick, but I'm tenacious, and I will break you." His voice was low and calm, and he could feel the edge. Then he stepped back. "And one other thing. Don't you ever discuss anything about me outside of the council again, not anywhere in this community."

Then he started down the hall, and he glanced back only once to see Hal walking the other way. At the reception, Mark took in the young girl Hal had somehow managed to point all the evidence toward.

"You all done, Chief Friessen?" she said, looking up from behind the laptop she was typing on.

"I am. Thanks, Jennifer."

She smiled brightly. "Have a good day, Chief."

"You too, Jennifer," he said, then walked out the door, wondering if that young lady, the assistant to a bunch of sleezy politicians, had any idea that they could and would set her up to take the fall to save their own skin.

God damn. Sometimes he really hated this job.

Chapter 8

New families, follow-ups, complaints, and telling Grant only what he wanted to hear. So much about this job took a piece out of her little by little. Maybe that was why Billy Jo was sitting in the dark in her small office with the blinds closed, needing a minute before she figured out which tasks she could push to the side and avoid and which she had to do.

There was a tap on the open door, and she dropped her hands from where they were pressed over her face and turned in her chair to see Gail, with her graying shoulder-length hair. She had never been in her office before.

"Gail, what are you doing here?"

"You busy? So this is where you hang out. You don't like lights?" She wore blue jeans and a blue striped T-shirt, the same one she'd worn earlier, with a brown purse slung over her shoulder.

"Come on in. I prefer the dimness when I'm trying to clear my head."

Gail didn't wait for her to say anything else. She closed the door and took a seat on the sofa. "Okay, you know that I like you—a lot," she started. "I think you're one very cool lady, and I've always been in your corner…"

Billy Jo just stared as Gail leaned forward, resting her arms on her legs, her hands linked, and then gestured to her. Something was wrong. "Okay…sure," she said, wondering what bomb was about to be dropped on her next. "Are you here to warn me about something, or what is this? Because I have to say, this feels very cloak and dagger."

Gail let out a heavy sigh. "You and Mark kind of remind me of Tolly and myself way back when. I was the girl who was going to right the world, idealistic, a dreamer. I backpacked across Europe into countries you wouldn't dare set foot in today, and I wasn't scared of anything. So when I tell you something, I need you to listen very closely. Sometimes you meet someone and know they're trouble, but you're naive. You believe right always wins in the end, and the good guy and bad guy are easily recognized and defined. But when the bad guy is the one making the decisions, in charge, the one everyone has to follow, lines begin to blur. Who is the criminal? You find yourself questioning everything about your community, how the rules are supposed to work. You know what I mean."

Billy Jo was speechless. "Gail, honestly, I have no

idea what you're talking about. Does this have anything to do with Ash or Sunday Byrd?"

Gail looked to the door, which was now closed, and pulled in a breath. Gail was smart, not coming right out and saying what was on her mind.

"Gail, you know I was adopted, and my dad worked as a fixer in Washington for politicians who found themselves in trouble. But at the same time, he's one of the best legal minds around, and he taught me about how laws work, how they're created, how the lines are blurred when people have power over other people. I have to wonder if you're scared or—"

"I'm smart is what I am, and I know you're an intelligent girl," Gail cut in. "Because you know as much as you do, you'll understand what I'm going to say next, and you're going to really listen. Tolly and I have managed to stay under the radar, so to speak, because we understood that for some people out there, fixing a problem is as simple as making a call, and no one will look into it. Ash Byrd is very much adept at solving problems, making them go away.

"Let's take a scenario. Say a woman has her sights set on getting close to a man, and not just any man but an athlete or a big-time celebrity that women flock to. Say he slips and sleeps with her, and oops, she accidently gets pregnant. But this big-time celebrity is married, and he can't have that problem. So his agent, manager, or lawyer makes a call to Ash to make the problem go away. Ash pays a visit to this confused woman, and he gives her a reason not to do what she's doing. Maybe she'll go running and tell her family or a friend, because she's scared, or maybe she'll tell the police if she's really stupid, so then Ash has to deal with the other people, the friends, the parents, the cops who shouldn't be looking too closely, and he has to take care of them.

"One thing about Ash is that he takes the reasonable approach first, as long as you follow the rules as he's clearly outlined them for you. But when you start dragging other people into the problem, it makes it difficult for him, and he starts doing things the hard way. Now he has to give these other people reasons not to do what they're doing, too."

Not once in all the time she'd known Gail had she ever seen her like this, looking around as she talked. She wondered if this was paranoia.

"Who is this guy, exactly, that he can do what he does?" Billy Jo said. "What, is he a former cop or something?"

Gail unclasped her hands and sat up straighter, pressing one to her thigh. "Cops do not ever have the kind of training he has. That knowledge and skill is something you learn only in the military, and not just as an average grunt. Ash spent years learning every skill, from explosives, to wiretapping, to psychological warfare—you know, to get someone to do what he wants and needs them to do. He understands exactly how to influence public opinion, how to master people's behavior and get them to bend, and he knows how to break them. You get what I'm saying?" Gail didn't pull her gaze, as if she was willing her to understand.

"You're saying Mark could find himself under investigation. I know he mentioned charges of sexual assault against a minor. And if he keeps fighting and trying to do the right thing, he'll have other charges and allegations coming from everywhere, old girlfriends, acquaintances, maybe people he's never met before. It'll be so bad that there's no going back, and his life will be over."

Gail slid forward. "As I said, you're a smart girl, and you love that guy. And he is a good guy, with a strong moral character, someone I would want in my corner—but not in this. You get him to walk away."

As Gail stood up, Billy Jo wondered if she had any idea what she was asking. "You realize Mark can't be bought or pushed around. The reason he's here is because he wouldn't look away from a bunch of dirty cops when he was told to. He's not going to back down, and I couldn't ask him to park his integrity and morals even if I wanted to."

Gail let out another heavy sigh and reached into her bag to pull out a folded piece of paper. "How did I know you would say that? Fine, here." She held it out.

Billy Jo knew she was frowning as she unfolded it, seeing a handwritten name, Amy Holt, and a phone number. She gestured to the paper. "What is this?"

Gail had one hand on the doorknob and the other on the strap of her purse. "Memorize it and then shred it. Do not share that name with anyone. Sometimes, when a woman finds herself in trouble, the kind of trouble no one can help her get away from, she gives the help that's needed."

She flicked her gaze to the name and number again. "Gail, please, are we talking about Sunday, the same girl you told me to steer clear of, the girl you warned me is a big storyteller?"

Gail looked at her in a way that said everything. "Sometimes a woman has to disappear for her safety, and for her children's, because she isn't safe where she is."

"So you're saying Sunday is in trouble and needs help?" She was leaning forward.

Gail shook her head. "My default position has always been to believe every woman, but not every allegation is real. Issues with accusations can make people run to opposite corners after an assault, especially when someone involved is in the public eye. Then things go horribly wrong. Liberal groups generally believe the woman, whereas more conservative groups believe the accused man. Listening to a woman recount such horrible intimate details is not pleasant, as I'm sure you know, and making a claim like that brings the kind of attention most women don't want to bring to themselves.

"So most accusers don't lie—but some do, and when someone does make a false accusation, it's a slap in the face to every woman who has faced the uphill battle of getting the police, the prosecutors, and the public to believe her, and it can bring down all the decades of progress we've made. So no one wants that lie made public. When an allegation is made, before evidence is even provided, people will blindly believe one side. Some go into a crazed fervor, ready to tar, feather, and burn the accused at the stake instead of waiting until the facts are in. Then there are the few who will never believe a woman, who will question her more than is becoming.

"Tolly was pulled into a rape case before he was chief. It was a he said, she said, where he said it was consensual and she said otherwise. After months of Tolly investigating, she ultimately admitted she had falsely claimed that consensual sex was rape after her boyfriend found out about her affair, which she had been hiding."

Billy Jo didn't like hearing this. Maybe that was why the earlier tension had returned. She pulled her hand across her face and looked over to Gail. "So she was outed by her boyfriend? Wow, a shitty thing. I bet the guy she accused has sworn off women forever. Who is she?" She wondered if Gail would tell her.

"She's gone now, left the island. He served seven months behind bars because his lawyer convinced him to take a deal and plead it down so he had some chance of a future. A day later, she admitted her lie, and Tolly was the one who spent months fighting the DA and the courts to clear Roddy Peepgrass's name," Gail said. When Billy Jo frowned, she gestured toward her. "Yes, the very same Roddy who owns the tow trucks on the island. Married now and has two teenagers, but I think the people who remember that day still believe he's not as innocent as he claims. That shadow of a doubt follows someone. Don't know why he stayed. Out of pure stubbornness, I think, refusing to be chased away from his home.

"Bily Jo, I'm telling you this because Mark won't survive a battle with Ash. Yet you already know you'll never convince him to walk away, to look the other way. You probably couldn't love him if he did, could you?"

She just stared at Gail, who seemed to understand her too well. "So why Amy? What is she going to do for Mark?"

Gail shook her head. "She's not doing anything for Mark. You're going to get her to help Sunday."

"You've lost me. Are you saying she's telling the truth?"

Gail let out a rough sigh. "No, what I'm saying is Amy is Mark's 'get out of jail free' card. If Sunday isn't here, then Mark has no case to look into. Sunday showing up the way she did means she hasn't been able to leave Ash, so her only way to leave is with the help of someone like Amy, who can help women disappear and never be found."

She hadn't expected this from Gail. Maybe there was a lot more to her and Tolly than she understood. "You're talking about women in abusive relationships with men they can't get away from…"

"Now you're starting to get it," Gail said. "Like the woman who's married to a cop and can't even report him because his friends are cops, so she'll never get help. Or the woman who's married to a judge, so not even the DA would be so suicidal as to go up against him. Or the woman married to any man who operates in the world of power. Amy creates safety plans and has access to new identities, an underground network only for women who have no other options. Memorize and then destroy that paper, and when you call her, tell her Vera Scott sent you."

Then she pulled open the door. Billy Jo wanted to ask who the hell Vera Scott was, but before she could, Gail said, loud enough that Pam could hear, "See you and Mark for dinner Friday. Tolly has been brewing his homemade beer and can't wait to have Mark as his first victim."

Then she walked away. Billy Jo heard her say something to Pam out front, and laughter followed. She stared at the name and number, reading them over and over to burn them to her memory, before getting up and walking to the shredder by her cabinet.

When she shoved the paper in, his image popped into her mind, the red hair, the arrogance, and the flaws. Damn, she didn't just care about Mark Friessen; she was totally, completely head over heels in love with him. So now she had no choice but to do everything she could to protect him from himself.

Chapter 9

He dumped his keys on his desk without a word after walking back into the station, trying to wrap his head around a cluster-fuck that seemed to be imploding around him.

"I take it that didn't go well," Carmen said as she strode in.

He looked past her to the two new cops he hadn't hired. "You want to say you warned me?"

She pulled her arms over her chest, and his gaze flicked to the deputy badge tucked into her jeans. A job she'd earned was being yanked from her. "So what am I supposed to do with those two? I have rounds."

He pulled in one breath and then another, his hands on his hips, then shrugged out of his jean jacket and tossed it over the back of his chair. He didn't know why, but he sat and reached for his keys, selecting the one for the bottom drawer.

"Tell me about those two out there," he said.

The lanky guy was sitting at his old desk, and the

lady walked out from somewhere in back and leaned against it, saying something to him. Lucky, meanwhile, was asleep, curled up on the dog bed.

"Dwayne Green, and the girl is Roberta Underwood. So I take it they're staying?" Carmen said as if she already knew the answer.

"Do you want me to say you're right? Never honestly saw this coming from the council," he said as he shoved his key in the lock of the bottom drawer and pulled it open only to see it empty. His ears were ringing.

"Chief, everything okay?" Carmen said.

He heard the door to the precinct, and he shut his eyes, closed the drawer, and looked up to see Billy Jo walking in. "Yeah, fine, sorry. Listen, was someone in my office?"

Billy Jo wore the same loose V-neck and blue jeans as she stepped into his office. "Everything okay?" she asked, likely from the expression on his face. Her gaze lingered as she dumped her bag on the empty chair.

Carmen looked over to Billy Jo and then back to him. "No one was in here. Why?" she asked.

"Someone has been in my desk. You sure one of them wasn't in here?"

Billy Jo stepped around the desk. She said nothing, but the way she glanced to the drawer and back to him, he wondered if she knew.

"No. I mean, I went to the bathroom, but I wasn't gone long enough. I told Dwayne to fill up the dog's dishes with food and water. Other than that, he's just been sitting at that old desk of yours. And Roberta has organized the pens and basically chatted it up with Dwayne. What's missing?" She frowned.

He forced himself to shake his head. "You know what? It's fine. And I'll deal with those two out there. Go do rounds, but when you get back, dig around and find out anything and everything you can on Sunday Byrd—her birthdate, her parents, where in California she's from… I want everything."

He could feel Billy Jo watching him intently, and when he looked up to the girl who had stolen his heart, her unsmiling blue eyes met his.

"Okay…" was all Carmen said as she started out of his office.

Billy Jo closed the door and walked back over to his side of the desk to sit on the edge. She was so close to him that her leg brushed his. Her back was to the door. "So is it what I think it is that's missing?"

Mark hadn't bothered to lock the drawer again, considering it was empty. He pulled it open, and she nodded as she looked down but said nothing. She glanced over her shoulder to the two newbies out front and back to him.

"And who are they?"

"Interesting you should ask," he said. "Remember the resumes I had you looking at yesterday, the ones marked by council? Well, those are the new hires, walked in by Hal Green this morning before I got here. Seems they signed a contract. The council had no intention of leaving it in my hands. Just got back from paying a visit to them. Went a round with Mary Jane and Hal, who also pointed out that one of them is taking over as detective, and Carmen is back to being a deputy with reduced pay. But she doesn't know it yet, and I haven't figured out how to deal with this. Worse, Hal mentioned the missing funding Herb was helping himself to. Seems it was an error, and they're ready to point the finger at their assistant, the girl who works the front desk."

Billy Jo's jaw slackened, and she pulled her arms over her chest. "You think they found out what was in your bottom drawer and helped themselves? Who has access to this office? How would they know?"

He pulled in a breath and let it out, staring at this girl he trusted more than anyone. "You know, after I walked out of the council office, realizing war had been declared, I climbed into my Jeep and thought of the photos of Mary Jane with Philip Maddox, the emails from Hal Green ordering the chief to take care of all his tickets, and the evidence of Herb Walker dipping into the local funding, all the dynamite that would have been enough to blow up their careers, which the chief had used to keep them in line. I never wanted to operate that way, Billy Jo. And as I was sitting there, watching, you know who walked into the council building?"

Her mouth was tight, her lips firmed. She uncrossed her arms. "Let me guess. Ash Byrd."

Evidently, she was smarter than he was, because he still couldn't believe he had seen that man walk up to the front door and inside. It only solidified that feeling he had that this was a game of cat and mouse —and he'd never expected to be the mouse.

"Maybe I should have asked you first," he said. "But now, seeing this drawer, I'm not surprised everything is gone. For all I know, Ash broke in here and helped himself. Is he working with the council? Maybe they hired him to take care of me, and I'm on my way out."

She shook her head. "Yet you're still investigating Sunday—or, rather, you're having Carmen do it. Did you forget his warning to you, Mark? Maybe, after seeing that empty drawer and seeing Ash walk into the council office, you need to take a step back. You have nothing to protect yourself." She lifted her hands and pressed them to her nose. He could see she had something to say, and he wondered whether he wanted to hear it.

"You want me to look the other way and refuse to help someone? I can't do that. If a crime has been committed, I'm going to investigate. No one gets a pass because of who he is. Sunday said he killed her family. You know what? Enough of this dancing around." He reached for his keys and stood up, brushing Billy Jo's leg. She was so close, and alarm flickered in her eyes as she looked up to him.

"What are you doing, Mark? Where are you going?"

He lifted his hand to skim her chin, running his thumb over it, and she wrapped her hand around his wrist, holding him there. "I think it's time to drive over and walk right into the lion's den, to see Sunday. Maybe, if I'm lucky, I'll have a few minutes to talk to her and get the story before Ash gets home." He pressed a kiss to Billy Jo's forehead, then stepped around the desk and pulled open the door.

"Mark, wait," she snapped, slipping off the desk and reaching for her purse. "I'll come with you."

He shrugged. "Well, let's go then," he said, and he started walking.

In the bullpen, two pairs of eyes looked over to him, and his dog was slurping water. Dwayne was appearing too comfortable in the chair he sat in.

"Dwayne, is it?" Mark said, stopping right in front of him.

The young man stood up. "Yes, Chief. Do you have something for me?"

He looked over to Roberta, who was standing by the open file cabinet, reading a file—a case file. He walked over, reached for it, and took it from her hands. "When I said touch nothing, I meant it," he said, then closed up the file and dumped it on the desk. "You keep an eye on my dog. He doesn't go out. Answer the phones and take messages. Any problems, you call me or Carmen."

He pulled open a drawer at Gail's old desk and pulled out two cards, one with his cell phone number and one with Carmen's. "You, over there," he said to Dwayne. Billy Jo was now standing right behind him. "You just sit there and do nothing," he said. Then he walked to the door and pulled it open, holding it and letting his girl walk out first.

"Chief, you want us to do nothing?" Dwayne called out.

Something about these two council picks only added to his growing unease.

"You heard me, nothing. Answer the phone and take a message, and if it's important, call me or Carmen. Pretty straightforward. Let's see if you can follow directions," he said before pulling the door closed behind him.

Billy Jo was already at his Jeep and had climbed in, and he pulled open the door and got behind the wheel, seeing how perfectly she fit with him. "You know, Mark, you're going to have to put them to work."

Another reason why he loved her. She was a voice of reason.

"Maybe so, but right now, I have a more pressing problem."

She was looking right at him and said nothing, so he backed up and put his Jeep in gear. Then she said in a soft, determined voice, "And what if Ash is there when we get there?"

He changed gears, slipped his sunglasses on, and pulled onto the road heading out of downtown. "I'll figure that out when I get there, but I'm not about to be told how to police my island."

She said nothing else. She didn't nod, didn't agree. Instead, she slipped on her sunglasses, looked straight out the window, and appeared rather calm and settled. But he knew one thing well about this woman. She didn't just go along with anything. Her being pensive and quiet meant she was thinking and planning.

Chapter 10

Sitting in the passenger seat of Mark's Jeep, riding in silence, was anything but uncomfortable. Being with him was easy in so many ways. Billy Jo took in the winding long driveway after the electronic gates that had opened automatically, ending in a huge two-story house with lots of glass and brick.

"No one's sneaking up on anyone here," Mark said as he pulled up and parked in front of the house by a three-car garage. The driveway was stone pavers, and the front door was all glass. Mark turned off the Jeep and stepped out, and she followed him, slipping her purse over her shoulder and sliding her sunglasses off as she took in the carving at the front door, a bear and an eagle. Everything about this place screamed money, wealth.

"Nice place," she said as Mark pressed the doorbell. She heard the chime inside, then footsteps, and she had to fight the urge to reach over to him. "Before we go in, please, for me, tread carefully," she said.

She'd never pleaded with him, and she didn't know what to make of the way he was looking at her as he lifted his sunglasses and settled them in his red hair. When the door opened, there was Sunday Byrd, wearing cut-offs and a lowcut tank, with a baby on her hip.

"What are you doing here?" she said.

Billy Jo couldn't pull her gaze from the baby, seeing the dark hair, the soother it was sucking on, wearing just a white T-shirt and a disposable diaper.

"I need to have a word with you," Mark said. "Is Ash here?"

Billy Jo wasn't sure if she would answer, as she just stood there for a moment. She could see Sunday was doing her best to pull it together, considering she couldn't hide how thrown she was.

She shook her head. "No, he's out, but he could be back anytime. You shouldn't be here."

Mark did something she didn't expect. He put his hand on the door and pushed it, making Sunday step back, and he stepped inside. "We have enough time to talk. You know who was waiting in my office this morning? Your husband, and he seemed to know all about your dropping by last night. Did you tell him?"

Billy Jo was now inside, as well, her hand on the door. Sunday was holding her baby, standing in the wide open entry, with its high ceiling, an open-concept living room behind her. When Billy Jo closed the door, she spotted a kitchen off to the left, huge and impressive, with so much light from the floor-to-ceiling windows. She figured a house of this magnitude had to run at least in the range of five to six million, easy.

"He asked me where I was, and I knew when he asked that he already knew, so yes, I told him I was at your house and drove out to see you," she said, then poked her tongue into her cheek, not pulling her gaze from Mark. When she glanced over to Billy Jo, she had to remind herself she didn't need to like this girl to help her. But as she looked around, nothing about this place screamed that the girl was in trouble.

"And you told him what, exactly, to explain your visit?" Billy Jo said, not looking Mark's way. "Because somehow, I don't think you told your husband that you drove all the way out to the chief's because you wanted his help to get away from him, from all this."

This wasn't a scared girl, she thought, but the way Sunday tightened her mouth reminded Billy Jo of herself before her dad found her and saved her. She wouldn't admit any of that to Mark, though.

"You don't know anything about my life," Sunday said. "You don't know anything about me, but here you are, standing in my living room, looking down your nose at me, judging me. You know, I could tell my husband you're harassing me, flexing your position as a social worker, saying you'll take our babies, and he'd see you off this island. Your job would be gone. So don't fuck with me."

Billy Jo wasn't sure if she hissed in response or whether that was the sound of the car she heard driving up. She didn't need to look to see that Ash was evidently home. Sunday stared back at her with smugness, and she wondered what she'd say. Lie or not, this was a sixteen-year-old who could destroy anyone.

"What is it that you want, Sunday?" Mark said. "Is this really about your parents, the ones you say Ash killed, or is this a game? And don't ever talk to Billy Jo like that again."

The door opened.

"Chief Friessen, to what do I owe the honor of this visit?"

Billy Jo took in the man, his neat short dark hair, average height and build, dark dress pants and white golf shirt. He was tanned and had dark eyes.

Ash walked over to Sunday and the baby she was holding and lifted it from her arms, squealing, to kiss on the cheek. He handed the baby back. "Willa asleep?"

Sunday nodded. "Yeah, but she's fussy again."

Billy Jo was waiting for the demand, the hysteria, the story from Sunday. Ash pressed a hand to her cheek, and she leaned into it as if loving his touch. She found herself looking over to Mark, who she could see was as confused as she was.

"Go check on her and put Sammy down," Ash said. "We'll have a late dinner tonight."

She walked out of the living room, barefoot, slender, up the stone steps to an open mezzanine and down a hall. Ash watched her, then slowly turned back, his gaze going right to Billy Jo. He said nothing for a second.

"So what brings you here, Chief? Either of you want an espresso?" He strode past them into the kitchen. The island was light stone, the cabinets modern oak, and he walked to an espresso machine and glanced back to them.

"Sure, why not?" she found herself saying.

"None for me," Mark said, an edge in his voice. "Impressive house you have here. You divide your time between the island and whereabouts in California?"

Billy Jo was now standing at the island, listening to the whir of the espresso machine. She glanced back to Mark and took in the high ceilings.

"You mean Tolly didn't tell you?" Ash said.

Billy Jo had to fight the urge to look back at Mark as Ash slid a small espresso cup in front of her. She'd expected him to make one for himself, but apparently, she was drinking alone.

"Thank you," she said, but he didn't even look her way, giving everything to Mark.

"Hollywood Hills," he said. "Sunday will be heading back earlier than usual with the kids. But I don't think you're here to talk about where I live."

Right to the point.

"You're right, I'm not. You showed up in my office and gave me a warning about your wife, your sixteen-your-old wife, knowing she came to see me last night. Now it seems something of mine has disappeared, and, lo and behold, I watched you walk into the council office today. So I have to wonder, what are you up to?"

Billy Jo reached for the espresso and fought the urge to look back at Mark. She hadn't expected this slip from him.

Ash smiled as he let his gaze slide over to Billy Jo. "You two are quite the cute couple. Tolly and Gail were right about that. You know, one thing about the chief, before he was forced out because of his stupidity, was that he knew how to get his job done without the council telling him how to police. No matter what anyone thinks, he did a lot of good things here for a lot of people, and he knew when to ask for help. Any gift for the chief was for the chief. It didn't get willed to you because you took over."

Something about the way Ash spoke made her want to pull Mark aside and tell him he had to drop this and walk away.

"Is this where you warn me again that the council doesn't like being backed into a corner and that I need to watch my back?"

Ash smiled again and laughed softly. "Sunday's parents, Desiree and Steve Jackson, were planning on visiting, which is one of the reasons Sunday is heading back early, so her parents can spend some time with their grandkids. But I'll be sticking around for a bit. It seems some unexpected work has come up. It's interesting, though, how Hal Green's niece is taking over as the lead detective. I know Tolly wouldn't have that, no matter how many ways Hal came at it. She headed up an antiterrorism unit in New York, worked her first three years undercover in narcotics, and she's racked up more of a resume than you. Highly overqualified to be a lowly detective on an island. Would have expected someone like her to be chief. Figure Dwayne will take over as deputy soon, and I heard the council was even talking about offering to keep Carmen on if she considers taking over the dispatcher job and running the office. She'll have to take another pay cut, of course, but you know, that's what happens when you let people fuck you over and you're suddenly at their mercy."

Billy Jo looked back at Mark, who had his arms pulled over his chest, not breaking Ash's gaze. "And how would you know all this?" she said.

Ash didn't glance her way, and she wondered if he didn't even consider her a problem. "You know, I was just a street kid," he said. "I joined the army because it was the only option I had other than stealing and dealing and then landing in jail. The army knows a lot about electronics, and I learned they do more audio surveillance than the Feds will ever know. When the Feds do a wiretap, there are laws in place. A judge signs off, and they can record only a certain amount before they have to shut it off. With a wiretap, you're recording both sides of the conversation, but there are also bugs that can pick up all the talk in a room.

"I've found that people only love you when they need you, and it's amazing the things people will say over a phone, in a room, when they think no one is listening. Tolly Shephard has a soft spot for you, Mark Friessen. The council is getting ready to make some changes here, and it's entirely up to you how you want to handle it. Either way, my wife is leaving." He pulled open a drawer in the kitchen and pulled out a thick orange manila envelope and rested it on the island. He pressed his finger to it and slid it slowly over to Mark. "I don't often give gifts, but when I do, it's for the right reason."

Billy Jo turned her head, hearing footsteps as Sunday walked back out and behind the island to stand beside her husband. Her makeup made her look older, and she looked right at Billy Jo.

"You get packed already?" Ash said.

"Not yet."

"Your husband said you're going back to California to visit your parents," Billy Jo said, and she expected a reaction rather than the calm way Sunday was staring back at her.

"That's right," she said.

Billy Jo reached for the envelope on the island and held it out to Mark. "We should get going."

Mark didn't take the envelope at first, letting his gaze linger on her. Then he did. "I guess we're done here," he said, and she wasn't sure if the anger she was seeing was directed at her or this situation. She started to the door, hearing Mark behind her.

"Take care, Chief," Ash said. "You need anything, give me a call."

As they walked out of the house, Billy Jo took in Sunday Byrd standing in the open door behind them, just watching her. Then she closed the door.

Mark tossed the envelope on her lap as he climbed into the Jeep. "You have any idea what the fuck that was?"

Billy Jo stared at the house as Mark started the Jeep and put it in gear. She lifted the sealed thick envelope and looked over to him. "I'd say Sunday is playing a dangerous game, and this here, I could be wrong, but I have a feeling this may be your way of taking back control of the island. Do you want me to open it?"

He shoved his sunglasses back on and drove down the winding paved driveway, saying nothing for a second as he pulled in a breath and then let it out. "Nope," he finally said. "If I can't do this job the right way, then I have no business doing it at all."

She realized he was serious, and he'd said exactly what she'd hoped he wouldn't.

Damn him for being too perfect.

Chapter 11

Mark knew Billy Jo wanted to open that manila envelope, and he was well aware that any other girl would have already opened it.

"Give me your keys, Mark," was all she said as he made coffee back at the stationhouse, taking a second to glance back to the two bodies doing nothing, Roberta and Dwayne. He found himself staring at them, just taking up space. Roberta was sitting on the edge of Gail's old desk, arms crossed, and Dwayne had made himself too comfortable in his old chair, leaning back and just staring his way.

He reached into his pocket and pulled his keys out, then handed them to Billy Jo, and he realized Roberta was walking his way.

"Chief, you have a minute?" she said. "I would like to have a word with you about what I'm supposed to be doing, as I'm currently sitting here with my thumb up my ass, looking after your dog, answering phones, and ignoring all the problems on this island when I should be responding to calls and arresting people, ticketing them, doing everything a good cop is supposed to be doing. This isn't a good use of my time." She was not as tall as Carmen, her eyes a shade of brown, and it appeared she wasn't scared in the least of challenging his authority.

"And what do you feel would be a good use of your time?" he said as he flicked on the coffeepot. He turned to Roberta and realized the deputy shirt she was wearing had a logo for the Roche Harbor Police on it, one he'd never seen before. Evidently, the council had left him out of more plans they had for his office.

"Well, you have me here answering phones when there's been a disturbance reported out on Fisher Road, a call of indecent exposure. Then we got a call from a woman who said she's been trying to rent a property, and the male who owns it told her to send naked photos and videos of herself so he could see if she was suitable. We've had two calls of possible animal abuse, one a young dog who spends all day, every day chained up outside alone. Then there was a possible break and enter, a theft of camping equipment. Also, two young guys at the south beach are drinking and smashing bottles, and an alarm is going off at a home on Gillespie—and I see the alarm has gone off a few times at that residence." She shrugged. "I pulled the file on the address. That's not to mention a fight on the roof of the school involving two youths and someone shot with fireworks. With all due respect, Chief, shuffling all these calls to one woman who is in over her head is both reckless and—"

"Are you finished?" He cut her off quite sharply, seeing a woman who was ready to go toe to toe with him.

"Well, that depends, *sir*." The sarcasm dripped, and he couldn't pull his gaze, knowing when he was being openly challenged. "Are you going to keep me parked at a desk, collecting dust, or let me actually do the job I was hired to do, curbing the civil unrest that seems to be rampant on this island because of sloppy policing and criminals who know the new chief doesn't have the manpower to do anything? Yet here I am, ready to go." She pulled her arms over her chest.

He realized Billy Jo was watching him from the doorway in his office. "You think I'm going to let you loose in my community, on the residents here, because you were walked into my precinct by Hal Green, a councillor who turns out to be your uncle? Tell me, Roberta, when you signed a contract with your uncle, did you expect to walk in here and do whatever you wanted? What exactly were you promised by the council before you came into my station?" He knew lanky Dwayne was still leaning back in the chair, watching and listening to this showdown.

"Well, your lead detective is now reporting to me, so I guess we can do this the easy way or the hard way," Roberta said. "My uncle has been dangling the carrot to me, offering up the position here. Chief, if I were you, I would be over the moon with the qualifications I have. I have more experience and have seen more things than you've ever had to deal with on this island, and—"

"You mean you have so much experience that you expect to take over as chief," he said, cutting her off.

Her mouth was still open as if she wanted to speak, and her expression said everything. Mark flicked his gaze over to Dwayne, who hadn't looked away. Roberta closed her mouth and firmed her lips, and he could see she didn't want to answer.

"Let me be clear," he said. "At this point in the game, you are not the detective in charge. Your what I tell you you are. Your uncle is a politician, not a cop, so he doesn't get to oversee how the law works here. And, so you clearly understand, your uncle is not above the law. As far as Detective Zarco is concerned, you watch your step. You are not her boss, and she is not reporting to you. She has more island experience than a big-city cop whose major accomplishment has been running undercover in narcotics and looking for terrorists, whose first instinct is to see the worst in people.

"This is a small island compared to the big city, where millions are jammed in with some of the worst of the worst in the world. You believe you can walk into this community without catastrophizing or falling back on profiling based on race and gender? Because the policing here needs to be modified to our conditions. Before I let you loose anywhere, you need to prove yourself to me and show me you will respect the people here first and foremost. These are people who live here, real people with complicated lives, complicated issues, and you need to understand that.

"Our two main problems here, out of which stem a lot of other problems, are mental illness and a lack of housing. The alarm going off on Gillespie is for a multimillion-dollar property that sits vacant fifty weeks out of the year and is owned by a Hong Kong resident. If you'd have read the report, you would know the alarm has gone off twenty-two times in the last thirty days because of faulty wiring. No one answers the phone at the management company, so the monitoring company for the alarm has been contacted and told to fix the problem. Which, if any, of these calls did you forward to Detective Zarko?"

Roberta blinked. "Well, I was assuming I would handle it, Chief."

"So you didn't call Carmen about any of these complaints? I noticed my phone didn't ring, either. When I left here, I was quite clear with you. Answer the phone, and if there's anything important, you call me or Carmen."

She said nothing.

Mark held out his hand. "Where are the messages? Give them to me."

She hesitated only a second, then walked over to Gail's desk, where he noted files stacked. It seemed she'd been looking through them. She handed him a scrap piece of paper covered with numbers he couldn't read and names and notes that made no sense.

"What the hell is this? Is this what you do in New York?"

"It's my Coles Notes version. It works for me."

He just stared at her, realizing she was serious, and gestured at the desk. "And all these files are out because…?"

"Since I'm doing nothing, I was getting myself caught up on the cases, anything that's been overlooked."

He wanted to snarl. This entire day was snowballing downhill, picking up speed until it could blow up in his face. But he reminded himself that he'd dealt with worse. "Put the files away. I'm not having you second-guessing anything when you can't even take a proper message. Less than ten seconds ago, you were on my ass about not being able to police. Well, congratulations. Neither can you, based on this mess. You! Get over here." He jabbed his finger at Dwayne, who quickly jumped up, maybe from the pissed-off expression on his face, which would have told anyone he was long past being reasonable.

"You two, put your heads together right now and get these messages written properly. I want a phone number, a contact name, the time and date the call came in, the address, and exactly what the emergency is. Start with the dog that's tied up. If that phone rings again, I don't want to see sloppy shit like this. A good cop would know better. You both have five minutes to do a one-eighty, or you can use that fucking door and leave. I don't give a shit what you signed with the council or who you're related to. Do you understand me?"

Roberta only nodded, and Dwayne reached for the paper and said, "Of course, Chief. I'll get it to you right away."

Then Mark walked toward his office, where Billy Jo was still staring at him from the door. He moved around her, his hand on her shoulder, and she said nothing as she closed the door. He kept walking around his desk, but he didn't sit. He needed a second to pull it together. He forced himself to breathe in and out.

"Are you about to tell me how off base I was and that I'm only making things worse for myself?"

She made a face and shook her head. "No, I'm completely behind you. She was out of line. The envelope is in your bottom drawer, by the way. So… Desiree and Steve Jackson, you know, the murdered parents of Sunday Byrd, are very much alive and well in California."

He pulled in a breath, doing his best to shake what felt like the island working against him. "You sure they're alive?"

She shrugged. "Why don't you let me check into it? That way you'll stay off Ash and the council's radar."

It would be easier, but then she'd be in the line of fire. "No, but thanks. I'll check it out and then deal with the rest of this crap. Dinner tonight…?" He looked at the clock and knew it would be a late one.

Billy Jo reached for her bag and slung it over her

shoulder. "I'll take Lucky with me. You finish up what you need to do here, and I'll figure out something for dinner for us."

She slid her hands over his chest and rose up on her tiptoes, then pressed her hands to his cheeks and kissed him softly. Then she pulled back. It was unexpected, and he just stared as she walked straight over to the door. She was wearing blue jeans that fit her nicely, and something else about her seemed so different.

When she pulled open the door, Dwayne appeared with a handful of notes, smiling at Billy Jo as he walked past her into Mark's office.

"Here are the messages, Chief," he said.

Mark glanced at the notes, the names, the numbers, something that made sense. "Roberta, get in here," he called out, then handed a message to Dwayne. "Get the animal shelter to pick up this dog, and stop in at this other address. Call Carmen now and tell her to get out to the beach and take care of the nuisance complaint."

Roberta stepped up beside Dwayne and said nothing.

"And you, Roberta, call back the lady about the landlord wanting her naked photos and videos, and get a statement from her. When you find out the landlord's name is Freddie White, who's had a dozen complaints filed against him from women trying to rent a place, find out if she gave him anything and whether he took money from her. Then you get the file on my desk, and I'll have a word with him again.

Then I want you to go into the database and find out everything you can about a couple in California, Desiree and Steve Jackson. They have a sixteen-year-old daughter named Sunday."

He took in the two cops, whom he still didn't have a clue what to do with. Both were standing and staring at him.

"What are you waiting for?" he said. Dwayne walked out of the office, but Roberta's expression told him she had something else to say.

"So what, exactly, do you want me to look for on this Desiree and Steve Jackson?" she said.

He glanced to the front door, where Billy Jo was walking out with Lucky. Damn, he really did love her. Maybe he should tell her so. Then he dragged his gaze back to Roberta. "Anything. What they do for a living, an address, a phone number, parking tickets, how many kids they have, any red flags of any kind. Find out anything and everything you can about what they've done in the last month. Then you give it to me and no one else."

Her face was an open question, but, to her credit, she only shrugged, walked to the door, and said, "Sure, Chief. I'll start working on it now."

Chapter 12

"You just stay right here. I won't be long," Billy Jo said, running her hand over Lucky. She had rolled the window down enough that a breeze was blowing in, and Lucky lay in the backseat of her new car as she stepped out at the beachside access, where she'd parked beside a sleek silver Jag.

She started down the narrow trail and steps that led down to a rocky beach, and there she was, her blond hair hanging in soft waves, blowing in the breeze. She wore a brown cardigan and blue jeans, her arms were crossed, and she was staring out at the waves crashing against the shore. Billy Jo walked carefully over the rocks to join her, and Sunday glanced only once her way. She was a few inches taller, slender, curvy, and her blue eyes were filled with something Billy Jo didn't understand.

"You're probably asking yourself why I said Ash killed my parents," she said.

That was one of many questions she had, among which was why Sunday had called, wanting to meet with her, the minute she climbed in her car with Lucky.

"Well, you called me out here to explain. I don't understand why you showed up at the chief's with that story. You know your husband paid him a visit and warned him off, and I have to wonder if you had your hand in any of what he alluded to. I think you know what I'm talking about, the implication that Chief Friessen might suddenly find himself under investigation for sexual impropriety with a sixteen-year-old. You." She really emphasized the last part.

The ocean rustled Sunday's hair as she said nothing in response, just looking out.

"So tell me, Sunday, was any of that bullshit story you told us when you knocked on Mark's door true?"

This time Sunday looked right at her. "Some. My mom was working in Hollywood, and she did find herself in trouble, but it was the other way around. Ash was the one getting her out of the hot mess she'd found herself in. You know, most people have no idea that in Hollywood, you can get access to things no one else can. I remember hearing that in one of my earliest memories. I met so many big-time Hollywood players who came through because they had a problem, from a high-profile divorce, to being outed as gay, to drugs, sex, and gambling. He even scared off a few reporters who were hassling this big star. They were always being caught doing things they shouldn't have been doing, and I'd hear everything as Ash listened to their whining, their freaking out.

"He had an open door, as he said. 'You come to me with a problem, I solve the problem, and you pay me, but if you lie to me, you're dead.' You know, every one of those Hollywood elites knew I was just a kid, yet when they realized I was his wife, they smiled and said nothing. I could see the envy in their eyes, a few of the men. When I told him I was leaving him, before I had Sammy, he said the only way I would leave was six feet under.

"Ash records every meeting, every conversation, and all his recordings are encrypted. He knows how to terrorize someone, how to turn your life upside down so your personal information is no longer your personal information. If someone was causing a problem, he'd do anything and everything until that person could barely function. He'd run them off the road, make threatening phone calls in the middle of the night, cut their brakes, slash their tires, even disengage a locked electronic gate and disarm their security. I know he made sure explosives were planted in one's office, and a tip was called in to the FBI. The C4 and grenades they found were enough for federal charges, and the guy was locked away. So I know when he says six feet under, he'll never let me go." She was looking right at Billy Jo, young and old at the same time.

"Does he hurt you?"

Sunday only stared at her. "He has a girlfriend

down in San Diego. I have no idea why he wanted me."

"You're not answering me. Does he hit you, hurt you?"

She smiled and let out a laugh. "No, Ash is the perfect gentleman. He just doesn't share what's his with anyone."

What the hell did she mean by that? Billy Jo had to remind herself that everyone had a story, even though she wanted to turn around and walk away. "So you want to leave Ash, is that what this is about? What about your parents? Can you not call them and go home?"

The way she looked at her again reminded Billy Jo of the unfeeling adults who had hurt her when she was just a kid. "Steve and Desiree care only about Steve and Desiree. They were the ones who took me to Ash and okayed this sham of a marriage. They took away my freedom, and now I'm stuck in this hell and can't do anything. Yes, I want to leave and get as far away from him as I can so that he can't find me or our kids."

Billy Jo could feel her anger. "So you want to disappear. You know, Chief Friessen doesn't know you're meeting me here, and your going to him only put a target on him. I have to know, are you suddenly going to accuse Mark of something that could destroy him?"

She smiled and shook her head. "No, that's more Ash's style, not mine. I heard the new chief was the kind of guy who didn't look away when someone needed help and that he had a thing for the island social worker, you. Seeing you at his place when I knocked on the door, I have to say I didn't expect that. He's a very handsome man, attractive…"

Billy Jo crossed her arms over her chest and fisted her hands. "Is this a game to you? Because you're not messing with him. You may be married to Ash Byrd, but I'll take a chunk out of you if you do anything, say anything, or tell any lies about Mark. I may not be on your husband's level, but I do know how to fight, and I will come out swinging for someone I love."

Sunday actually lifted her hands and laughed as she stepped back. "Whoa, there. Cool off. I get it: He's yours, and you don't want anyone messing around with him. I just want to leave Ash. And my parents, they can go straight to hell."

Billy Jo dragged her gaze back out to the waves, then nodded as she glanced back to Sunday. "You would've set up Mark with no remorse if your husband told you to."

She supposed anyone else would have denied it, but Sunday only blinked, far too calm. "It's too bad that you happened to be there when I knocked on the door," she said, and the knot in Billy Jo's stomach tightened as she stared at a teenager who didn't seem to have an ounce of empathy.

"Keep your phone on. I'll make a call. But, Sunday, when you leave, disappear. I don't ever want to hear from you again."

Then Billy Jo walked back to the stairs and started up them. When she reached the top, she looked back at the teenager, a shell of a girl who should have been innocent. As she stared at Sunday Byrd, the pieces were falling together: the lying, the lack of remorse or empathy. She figured if she looked closer into the girl, she might also find that she was cruel, manipulating and hurting others, with no idea of right and wrong. Mark would walk right into her trap, doing anything to help her, and when he figured out what he was dealing with, even Billy Jo wouldn't be able to save him.

She lifted her cell phone, and it rang only once.
"Hello?"

She watched Sunday shove her hands in her sweater pockets, and she thought of Gail, who'd given her this number.

"Hello," Billy Jo said. "Vera Scott sent me."

"Tell me where you are."

She nodded, wondering what Gail knew about Sunday that she didn't, and she turned away and started up the trail to her car, rattling off her address. The woman hung up on her after saying she'd call her back, and Billy Jo pulled open the door and slid behind the wheel. Lucky kissed her face.

"Just one more stop, boy, and then we're going home."

Chapter 13

The chime of the doorbell had her holding her breath for a moment, and she reached down and ran her hand over Lucky, who was right beside her. When the door opened, staring down at her was a familiar unsmiling round face. The way he looked at her reminded her why she'd never liked Tolly Shephard.

"What are you doing here?" he said.

Okay, so now it was awkward.

"Hi. Is Gail here?" Billy Jo did her very best to put all the friendliness she could into her voice as she looked up at a man who had never made a secret of how much he didn't like her, either.

He stepped back, then bent down to the dog. "Hey there, Lucky. Missed you."

At least the dog was welcome.

Tolly gestured to her. "Well, come on in," he drawled and stepped back. "She's in the kitchen, just getting dinner on."

Billy Jo slipped off her sandals and walked inside, and she heard Gail fussing over Lucky, who had walked right in. She followed the dog and took in Gail at the island with what looked like dinner preparations underway, a pot on the stove, a cutting board out, and a mix of vegetables cut up.

"Well, this is a surprise," Gail said. "What brings you by?"

Billy Jo found herself looking back for Tolly, but he wasn't there. She took another step back, angling her head to the front door.

"He's likely in his den," Gail said, evidently knowing what she was doing. She gestured to the front of the house. "Hides out in there more and more as of late."

"Well, remember your visit earlier to my office?"

Gail turned off the stove and gestured sharply for her to be quiet, pressing a finger to her lips. She walked to the back door and pulled it open, and Billy Jo followed her outside onto the deck. The dog had already gone out ahead and was down on the grass.

"Let's go for a walk," Gail said and started down the steps onto the grass of the backyard, which stretched out for a long way. The view of the ocean in the distance was breathtaking, and so was the privacy.

"So I met with Sunday Byrd," Billy Jo said. "She lied about her parents being murdered. I don't understand why she'd do it. She wants to leave him, though. I'm here because it seems as if I'm the only one who doesn't understand what's going on. I mean, come on, Gail. You showed up with all this cloak and dagger stuff, which is starting to weird me out a bit. I made the call, used the name…" She gestured widely.

Gail made a face and pulled her arms over her chest, looking down at her as they walked. "You know, this view never gets old. It was why we bought this place, why we built the house where we did. A wonderful place to raise the kids, growing up on the island in a small community where you know your neighbors. If someone does something, you know who it is. Just like in the big city, bad things happen to women in smaller communities, but we have even more strikes against us and nowhere to go."

Billy Jo found herself looking back to the house as they approached two red Adirondack chairs set up in the middle of the grass. She thought they'd sit, but Gail kept walking, taking her further from the house. "You warned me about Sunday. I guess I need to know why."

For a moment, Gail said nothing. They were closer to the edge of the yard, and she could see the valley and the ocean in the distance. "I heard you and Mark paid a visit to Ash Bryd," she finally said. "The phone rang right after you were there. Ash called Tolly, told him he gave Mark everything he needed to keep his job. Did Mark open the packet?"

Billy Jo stopped walking, taking in the privacy, wondering why it seemed she was in the middle of this game. "Of course he didn't. I locked it in his bottom drawer. Tell me about what's in there, because he won't use it, and I'm afraid he's going to be blindsided."

Gail pulled in a breath. "Everything the council doesn't want the public here to know. New cars, missing money, a rise in tax dollars redirected to them, and a funding program called Bill 33, which is basically a discretionary fund no one knows about that lines their pockets. There's a lot more in there, nothing they'll want to come out."

She just stared at Gail and wondered how she knew all this. "Mark won't use it, and you know the council already sent in those two…"

"You mean Dwayne and Roberta?" she cut in, and Billy Jo realized she really did have her finger on the pulse of the island.

"Yeah. Do I dare ask how you knew? Come on, Gail. I feel like I'm pulling teeth here. Help me out. Just tell me what to do, because Mark won't open the envelope or use it, and you know what? It infuriates me because I couldn't love him if he did."

Gail didn't look away, and for a moment, Billy Jo wondered if she was going to laugh at her. "Never figured he would, but the council doesn't need to know that. As far as Dwayne and Roberta, the council can show them the door, pay them off out of their discretionary budget. Roberta is here to take over Mark's job, but I'm sure you already know that. You make sure Mark hires his picks and stands his ground. About the council, Tolly has been meaning to drop by and catch up. You know, Billy Jo, there's one thing I know about Mark and his damn integrity, and that's that if he knows you did something behind his back, it would kill your relationship."

She pulled her arms across her chest, staring at the dog. "You really didn't want to talk inside."

Gail glanced back to the house. "You know, you think people are paranoid when they think someone is following them and listening in on their phone calls, saying the walls have ears. But sometimes they do."

A shiver ran down her back as she glanced back to the house and then to Gail.

"Ash Byrd is not a man you want to get on the bad side of," Gail continued. "Sunday means everything to him. Not sure what fucked-up reasoning her parents had to marry her to the man as young as she was, though. When she's gone, you make sure Mark stops looking. Ash will call him, but there won't be a trace of her."

"So this lady I called is…"

"A friend," she said, cutting Billy Jo off, "who has helped a lot of women who needed to disappear do just that." Gail pulled a weary breath and glanced away. "Where is she meeting you?"

Billy Jo lifted her watch and looked at the time. She needed to leave. "My place. I should get going. She didn't say much, just asked my address and said she'd be there."

Gail nodded. "I'll meet her. It's better you don't get involved anymore."

Billy Jo stared at her. "You're serious. Then what?"

"Then, when Sunday disappears, you can honestly tell Mark that you have no idea what happened to her." Gail slid a hand over her shoulder.

"And when are you going to stop the dancing around you've been doing with him, this question about his place, your place? Pick one!" There was the smile.

She fell in beside Gail as they walked back to the house, and she felt the fear that always came at her out of nowhere, but she kept walking. "You're telling me to take a leap of faith."

"No, I'm telling you to follow your heart. Good guys don't come along every day, and neither does the guy you know you'll spend forever with. But he won't wait forever."

Billy Jo nodded as she kept walking. She called out to Lucky, then spotted Tolly walking onto the deck. "In case I didn't say it," she said, "thanks for sticking your neck out."

Gail nudged her. "You're welcome."

Chapter 14

It was dark when Mark pulled in and parked in front of his cottage beside Billy Jo's Nissan. Light drifted through the windows, and he wanted to shut his eyes after the shitstorm of the day, but he spotted the door open, and there was Billy Jo, gesturing as if to ask what he was doing.

Damn, he didn't know if he had it in him to do any more dancing around tonight. They'd eat and then she'd leave. He pulled on his door and stepped out, then started up the deck toward her.

"Well, was wondering if you were going to sit out there all night," she said. "I made a meatloaf." She was barefoot, he realized, and let her gaze linger as she looked up at him. "Please tell me it got better after I left?"

He touched her cheek as he thought of the mess he'd left, papers scattered, when Dwayne and Roberta both walked out the door at five. He'd have said something, but he was still trying to figure out his next move, because he wasn't taking this lying down with the council.

"Well, let's see. Roberta managed to dig up a history on Sunday's parents, Desiree and Steve. They live in Pasadena. She dug up a phone number."

She was already inside and had walked over to the oven, and he breathed in the aroma of the meatloaf and watched as she lifted the casserole dish out and set it on his stove. Damn, he hadn't realized he was so hungry.

"You called them?" she said.

He wondered what she'd say when she heard the parents thought nothing was wrong with what they had done. "I did, and I asked outright if their sixteen-year-old daughter was married to Ash Byrd. You know what her mother said?"

Billy Jo didn't say anything. Mark still couldn't believe how badly the conversation had gone. "I'm taking it she wasn't supportive or worried about her daughter."

Mark shrugged out of his jean jacket and went to toss it on the sofa, where Harley was lying, his eyes closed, Lucky on the other end. When he glanced back to Billy Jo, she gestured toward him.

"Well, come on. Tell me, what did they say?"

He rested his jean jacket on the arm of the sofa and looked back to her. "Other than that she was an amazing storyteller, lied all the time, and thought nothing of hurting others? She told me they pulled her off the street after she started selling herself because she wanted an Xbox and they'd said no. She even went so far as to say that Ash married her as a favor to them."

Billy Jo said nothing, only nodded.

"You know, I can't help noticing you don't seem surprised."

She took a step toward him, then another, and rested both her palms on his chest. "What do you want me to say? I recognized something about her. I grew up in some really shitty places, and I've seen it before and been on the wrong side of that kind of person, the kind you can't trust with anything, especially your life. She could mess with you and you wouldn't even see it coming. So does this mean you'll leave it alone?"

What was he supposed to say? He was still bothered by the fact that she'd been thirteen when Ash married her. Billy Jo let her hands fall away and stepped back.

"Not much I can do," he said. "So I see Harley is here." He looked at the floor in the kitchen, seeing the cat's dish beside Lucky's. "And so is his dish. Does this mean what I think it means?"

He expected her to pull away, make a face, and get all uncomfortable, but she just looked at the meatloaf. He spotted a pot on the stove and a salad already made.

"You've been pushing me for so long to make a decision, and I'm sorry it took me this long," she said. "I figure I'll give my notice to Lesley and Lorne and move my things in here, or we could look for something bigger."

It took him a second to realize she was serious. He slid his arms around her, and she settled into him. "You sure about this?"

She angled her head, freckles dotting her face. Her blue eyes were so different from those of anyone he'd known. He lifted his hand, brushed back her hair, and leaned in and kissed her softly, then pulled back.

"More sure than anything in my life. But one thing, Mark."

He kissed her again, and she slid her hand over his chest. He pulled back just a bit and took in the seriousness of her gaze. "And that is?"

She slid her hand over his arm and up his sleeve, then stepped back as she lifted it. "You keep your appointment and get this removed."

There she was, his snarky Billy Jo.

Man, he really did love her.

Chapter 15

Mark slid his hand down her back as he sat on the sofa. She was straddling his lap, kissing him, feeling those warm lips, his hands sliding under her shirt and over her skin as she was pressed into his solid chest. She slid her hand over his face, feeling the scrape of whiskers, the same that burned her face now, and her other hand slid into his hair, the short unruly waves. She felt the strength of his solid thighs, melting into his touch, when his hand suddenly slid over her arm and he pulled her back abruptly.

"Okay, stop," he said.

Was he serious?

He was standing up, juggling her awkwardly, and she slid all the way down him, feeling every hard, uncomfortable inch. She swept back her hair, and his expression had the knot only twisting tighter in her stomach as she stood there.

"What are you doing? Why…?" was all she could

get out. She watched in horror as he paced in front of her, as if he realized he'd made a mistake or something.

"Look, as much as I want you—and let me be clear, I do, but I don't want to have you under me and then suddenly realizing you're in over your head or freaking out and backing away. This feels like walking into a trap. I don't want to complain, but, Billy Jo, we've been dancing around this 'us' thing for so long, and I've had to be patient and not push, and now all of a sudden you're here, and your cat is here, and you packed a bag and plan to stay over…but then what? Until you freak out again? I'm having a hard time believing you're suddenly comfortable enough to go all in."

She thought he was the one who sounded like he was freaking out. He paced, jammed his hands in his hair, and she didn't have a clue what to say to convince him.

"You know how I feel," he continued, "but you have so many triggers that sometimes I feel as if I'm navigating a minefield. Now you're suddenly good with everything?"

She realized he was serious. "I'm choosing not to let myself run and fall back into that terrified black hole of believing you can't love me. I'm trying here, so why are you suddenly the one pushing me away? I thought you really wanted this. You're the one who kept saying you wanted me here, and my cat. Did I overstep?"

His phone had started ringing before she could

finish, and he walked over to where it was lit up on the scratched square coffee table beside their empty dinner plates. He grabbed it, letting out a frustrated sigh. "This is Friessen…" He ran his hand over his hair, and when he turned, giving her his back, all she could see was his impressive strength and his faded blue jeans. Everything about him, the way he looked, the way he talked, was just under her skin.

"What are you talking about, gone?" he said, then turned back toward her and really listened to whoever was on the other end. She thought it was a man, and her stomach knotted, because he had shut his eyes in that way he did when he was frustrated and let out a sigh. "Don't do anything. I'll be right there," he said, then hung up.

Those vivid blue eyes went right to her as he held up his phone, then shoved it in his pocket. For a second, he didn't say anything. "That was Ash. Sunday is gone."

She stilled and felt her chest tighten. She'd forgotten to breathe. Mark walked around her into the bedroom and then back out, holstering his gun and his badge. He strode over to the sofa, where Harley was curled up, asleep, and reached for his jean jacket. When he pulled it on, she knew he was one step from walking out the door.

"Mark, wait."

Why the hell did she feel so damn guilty? Maybe because the one thing she knew about him was that honesty meant everything. "What are you planning on doing? You know she wanted to leave…"

She could see the frustration in the way he shook his head, and she wasn't sure he'd answer her as he gripped the doorknob, about to pull the door open.

"Nothing to do with it, Billy Jo. There was a call, so I'll get over there and find out what this is about. I'll look and see, and if there's evidence of a crime, I'll investigate. Being chief here, when a call comes in, I need to handle it whether I want to or not." He pulled the door open and took a step out. "I don't know how long I'll be…"

"I'll come with you."

He was already shaking his head, facing her as she walked over and reached for her brown cardigan and her purse from a hook at the door. "No, you stay here. I don't want you involved in this anymore. I don't want you on Ash Byrd's radar. In fact, I wish I could go back and undo your coming to his house with me, since now he knows about you."

She was already shoving her feet into her flats, and she stared up at Mark. He had to know she wasn't about to listen. "I'm a big girl, Mark, and have had to deal with worse. I'm not worried." She slid her hand over his chest and patted it as she slipped past him out the door, but he gripped her hand, holding her so she couldn't take one step further.

"I'm serious, Billy Jo. I'm worried. Do you have any idea what Ash is capable of? Because I do, and it's the kind of thing that would give you nightmares. With his wife missing now, I want him the fuck off my island, because this has shoved in my face just how dire this situation is, and I can't do anything about it because the law is on his side. How screwed up is that?" he said with passion, something else that drew her to him.

"I'm very well aware of how screwed up the law is. I spent too many years not being protected because the laws aren't made for kids like me. I'm well aware of all the antiquated laws still on the books that no one would ever consider enforcing, and I'm well aware that a bill that would have ended child marriage in California, where Sunday was married to Ash, ran into opposition from legislators. And you know what? No one cares. Well, not really. They're only horrified when it lands in their backyards."

She could feel the fury and wondered if he'd still tell her no. She knew he could sideline her now, though he'd never hesitated to take her into anything and everything before.

"Please, Mark."

He gestured and let out a sigh. She could see and feel how this was taking a toll on him. "Well, let's go. But hear me, Billy Jo. Say nothing. I don't know what the hell is going on, but I have a bad feeling about all of this."

IT WAS FULLY DARK when he pulled up in front of the massive house with light spilling from all its windows, as if every light inside was on. Mark parked in front beside a white pickup she knew was Gail's and a fancy black SUV.

Mark had said not one word to her on the way over. She just gestured to the truck, and all he did as he turned off the Jeep and stepped out of the vehicle was grunt. She followed him, leaving her purse in the Jeep.

He looked inside the white pickup and shook his head. He was really moving.

"You know that's…"

"Yeah, I know," he said, not letting her finish, as he started to the door. She found herself reaching out and gripping his arm because she could feel the secret she'd been keeping from him and the wedge it would drive between them.

"Before you go in, I need to tell you something."

The door opened while he was still looking at her with surprise, shock, and a frown. Then he dragged his gaze to the open door and Ash Byrd.

"About time you got here," Ash said as he walked back in, leaving the door open. Mark gave Billy Jo a quick glance as he walked inside, his cowboy boots scraping on the hardwood. He said nothing to her, and Billy Jo followed him, closing the door behind her. When she listened to the voices, she realized it was the chief there, not Gail.

"Look, just calm down, Ash," the old chief said in that way of his. "I'm sure there's an explanation here, like I said…"

When she realized the baby was still there, in a swing, going back and forth, her heart thudded. For a second, she stopped listening to what the chief was saying. The baby started fussing, kicking his legs, and

Ash leaned down and lifted him from the swing. She heard her breath loud in her ears along with the thudding of her heart. Sweat beaded down her back.

"Look, when did you last see her?" Mark had his notes out.

The chief looked over to her, letting his gaze linger, and she wondered if he knew. She kept her arms crossed and made herself look away.

"So you're telling me, Chief Mark, that you have no idea where she is," Ash said. "I mean, after that gift I gave you, I didn't expect this. She's gone. I came home and the kids were alone. Alone!" he shouted. "She left the babies, so that tells me something happened. Did you do this?"

She actually jumped from the way he shouted. The fire in his eyes reminded her he was not a man to ever cross. The baby wailed, and he walked over to the fridge and pulled out a bottle of formula, which he set in a bottle warmer on the counter. He shushed the baby, which she knew had to be around six months old. It was such a contradiction, going from cold fury to caring for a child.

"Yeah, don't go there," Mark said. "The last time I saw Sunday was here with you. I have my own shitstorm to deal with, so I don't need anything else added to my plate. What do you mean, the kids were alone? How do you know she left? For all you know, she could be out with friends."

Ash reached for the bottle and tested it to see if it was too hot, then slipped it into the baby's mouth, met with loud sucking noises. "Her closet. She packed her favorite clothes, and her suitcase is gone. All her makeup, her toothbrush, her personal stuff from the bathroom."

"She didn't leave a note?" Tolly said, pulling his arms over his chest again, his expression puzzled.

Ash only inclined his head, then let his gaze settle on Billy Jo, cold and unfeeling. A chill rose inside her. The way he looked at her, she remembered Mark's warning.

"If there were a note, you wouldn't be standing here. She didn't leave anything except her key to the house, which is sitting on the hall table by the front door as if she took it off her keychain. I'm not a fool. I go into enough situations that I know when someone is sending a message."

Mark glanced once back to her, and she wondered for a moment if anyone had any idea what she knew. But she couldn't believe Sunday had left the babies.

"I know you have surveillance," Mark said. "You're telling me you haven't watched it, haven't listened to the recordings you keep?"

Ash was almost vibrating with rage. "It was turned off, and not by me."

Mark said nothing, only looked over to Tolly, and she wondered if he was glad the old chief was there. Billy Jo was.

Damn, Sunday was a smart girl.

"You think someone was in here and turned it off?" Mark said.

Ash was watching the baby finish the bottle. "Oh, I guarantee you it was that sweet wife of mine. She knew too much but pretended she didn't. I want you to find her and bring her back." He was looking right at Mark, giving an order, a demand.

"You know it doesn't work that way, Ash," the old chief said. "Mark can only investigate if there's a missing person. If she left of her own accord, and that's what it's sounding like here, you know how the law works."

"You think I give a shit about the law? That's not why I called you here. You find her, you bring her back. That's how this works." Ash looked right at Tolly, then over to Mark, who was now shaking his head.

"You know, I hear your anger," Mark said, "but when a teenager who doesn't want to be married anymore runs off, it's not a police matter."

Tolly slapped his chest to cut him off, stepping closer. "What Mark means to say is that it can't officially be a police matter. But he'll look, and so will I."

"You'll find her is what you'll do." Ash leaned in again, his voice low, his warning clear.

"And then what?" Tolly said. "Come on, Ash. This is me. She's sixteen and she doesn't want to be here. You can't make her, because I won't drag her back against her will."

Billy Jo was very aware of how the old chief had stepped up as if he were running the entire show now, taking charge. She wanted him to take the spotlight off Mark.

"You just find her," Ash said. "You tell me where

she is, and I'll deal with her. What happens to her isn't your concern."

Tolly slapped Mark's chest again and moved him back, likely because even she knew that Mark wasn't having any of this. "Now, Ash, you just calm down. The kids are fine. She likely ran off to have some fun and will be back. Mark can run some searches for her and put her name out. But I don't want to hear anymore about your dealing with her. Mark, you want to have a look around?"

The way the chief spoke, it was as if Mark worked for him again. Billy Jo didn't miss the way Ash was watching her. He was sharp, smart, and could ruin everything and anything for Mark.

"Yeah, I was called in because your wife is missing. I want to see everything," Mark said.

"Let me give you a piece of advice there, Chief Mark," Ash said. "It's in your best interests to find her. And you'd better hope I don't find out you had anything to do with her slipping away, helping her leave. Her car is gone, and her GPS was disabled, so there's no doubt in my mind that she had help. Her coming to you, showing up at your house, toying with you the way she did, she was testing the waters, because that's what she does. You think I didn't know exactly where she was?"

Mark went to step around the chief, who was still standing there as if putting himself between the two men. "Well, it wasn't me. No matter what my personal feeling are, I'm very aware your marriage is legal. She lied about her parents being murdered. Yet

I can't shake the feeling that you two have some cat and mouse game going on, and I'm right in the middle, being jerked around. And I don't like that."

Ash only nodded. His eyes were dark and held a kind of ruthlessness. She realized this call was likely to figure out what Mark knew. She wanted to reach out and pull him back because she realized he wouldn't back down, even when Ash was beginning to gain a hold over him.

"You know what, Mark?" the chief said. "You've done all you can here. You and Billy Jo should head on out. Not much to see in the house. Ash and I have a few things to figure out."

"Hey, Chief, if it's all the same to you, no," Mark said. "I'm the chief of this island, and the last thing I'm going to allow is any vigilantism or anyone dragging back a girl who doesn't want to be here. And that's exactly what this is starting to sound like."

Billy Jo slid her hand over Mark's arm, and he dragged his gaze back to her. She could see his frustration. "Mark, Tolly is right. We should go."

"Ash, as I said, I'll look into it," Tolly said. "You know me. You know what I can do."

Mark didn't pull away from her, but she really could feel him digging in. Then the chief turned around and put his hand up to Mark, gesturing for him to go, and somehow he had Mark turned and moving toward the door.

"I'll touch base with you later, Ash," the chief called out.

Billy Jo pulled open the door and stepped out first,

and she could feel the simmering anger in Mark. Tolly only gestured for them both to keep moving as he closed the door, then walked over to his pickup.

"You stay out of this, Mark," he said. "I'm not kidding. You don't know Ash Byrd. You have an island to police."

"Excuse me, did you forget the part about my being the chief here, not you? You don't have any say here." Mark was really digging in.

Tolly shook his head. "That's right, so you have people here who depend on you not to be a hotshot, reacting in a way that could hurt so many on this island. This isn't a missing person, and you already know that. She left, and he'll soon realize it's for the best. He's got his kids. In this, you need to have your hands clean, Mark," the chief said, then looked around anywhere but at Billy Jo.

"Then why the hell was I called to come out here tonight?" Mark said. "Damn, I do not like feeling as if I'm being played with."

The chief looked right at him before letting his gaze finally linger on Billy Jo. "He wanted to be sure you weren't involved."

"And he knows that how?"

The chief had a way about him. Billy Jo realized now that she'd never really known him. "You can't hide anything, Mark. You have the worst poker face. He knows that. Go home. You've got a full day tomorrow, considering you need to staff that office."

Billy Jo dragged her gaze from Mark to the chief, who had pulled open the door to his pickup.

"What are you talking about?" Mark sounded pissed, and could she blame him? Not really.

The chief glanced over to Billy Jo again in a way that made her wonder how much he knew about her visit with Gail. "The council apparently saw the error of their ways and that they had overstepped. Roberta and Dwayne's contracts have been canceled. The council will mind their Ps and Qs. But you need to get people hired tomorrow for Gail's old job and the deputy position," the chief said, then nodded, slid in behind the wheel of Gail's pickup, and started it.

Mark looked back to her, and she could see the question there. "What the hell just happened? Or do I want to know?"

She ran her hand over his arm, glancing back to the glass front door, where Ash was watching them. Mark must have understood, as he walked around to his side and climbed in, and so did she. He started the Jeep, and she pulled her seatbelt on.

"You know, Mark, right now, can we please just go home? Whatever this was, I think maybe someone is watching out for you."

He put the Jeep in gear and followed Tolly Shephard down the long driveway. "You know, I wasn't born yesterday, Billy Jo, so how about telling me what the hell is really going on? Because before you went in, I had this feeling that you knew something about what the hell this mess was." He glanced her way with a look that could end everything good between them, then looked back to the road.

"You're talking about Sunday," she said.

"You need me to spell it out? I will. You know something about Sunday disappearing, where she is, and this thing with the council." He glanced over to her again, and her breath caught. She shut her eyes in the dark for a second.

"I won't ask again," he said.

She looked over to him. "Please don't be mad."

"If you don't tell me what the fuck is going on, Billy Jo, my being mad will be the least of your worries."

Right, his damn code.

"I don't know everything, but I do know she was leaving one way or the other, and someone was helping her. I don't know who. As for the envelope in your desk, the contents are the kind of dirt the council would never want public. As I said, someone is watching your back. I just wish I had been the one to do it."

Chapter 16

Billy Jo was sitting outside on the deck with Lucky, fussing over him, as Mark watched the cat hop down from the sofa and over to the bowl on the floor. He grabbed a beer from the well-stocked fridge and spotted the bottle of red, which she preferred chilled, so he pulled it out and reached for a glass on the shelf. He filled it halfway and then added some more before putting the wine back in the fridge, taking in the vegetables he'd never buy. He twisted off the cap of his beer and took a swallow.

"You stay in here," he said to Harley, who was munching on his kibble, then reached for the wine and walked outside, pulling the door closed behind him. He spotted Lucky's tail out in the long grass, and Billy Jo was sitting on the edge of the deck, her feet on the ground. She looked up to him in the dark as he approached. "Here you go, chilled."

She took the wine, and he just stood there, looking down on her, keeping the distance.

"I'm waiting." He gestured toward her. "You lied to me."

She took a swallow of wine, then said, "No. I just didn't tell you. But I don't know everything, and I'm glad I don't know everything. She left her kids. I didn't expect that." She stared out into the distance as she reached over and touched his leg. "Mark, this is hard enough. Don't put this distance between us. Sit down, because I don't want to keep looking up. I didn't lie, because I wouldn't lie, which is why I'm telling you now that Gail paid me a visit to warn me about Sunday, that she wasn't telling the truth. But we had fought about it already, and I was so angry at you because you swallowed her story even when I knew there was something wrong, because I was that girl who had been assaulted and had no one there for me. If my dad hadn't saved me, I wouldn't have had a future. She basically lied because she could, and I hate her for that. She may be a kid, but the way it rolled off her tongue…"

He stepped off the deck and rested his foot on the edge, just looking at her, seeing the emotions and knowing they were stepping right into all of her no-go topics.

"Do you know how young I was when I was assaulted the first time?" she said. "It was someone I knew, someone who was supposed to look out for me." She looked up at him, and he sat down beside her, looking down at her, and just waited. "You know some of it, but you don't know everything. I was nine years old." She made a face. "It wasn't just one foster family, either. Maybe I do see the worst before the best in people now, but there's something familiar to me in someone who has those kinds of antisocial behaviors, which I've seen only a few times. I knew there was something off about Sunday. When Gail came by my office, she told me that Sunday wanted to leave, and she gave me the name of someone to call, someone who helped women who needed to disappear." She looked over to him, and he realized she was serious.

"You're not talking about…"

"Mark, you're not a fool. You know there are women trapped in situations where justice won't work for them. They can't get away from the monsters they're married to, and those men will never leave them alone. A woman can end up hurt or dead, or if her husband has enough on his side, he can convince a judge to take her kids from her. You know it happens."

"So is that who you called?"

She took another swallow of wine, then scratched her head. "Sunday called me, and she met me down by the ocean. You know, she was rather proud of the way she had you believing her story about her parents. I'm not saying the other stuff isn't true, but to her, this was a game. Oh, she wanted to leave, though, and the fact was that her parents basically handed her over to Ash as a thirteen-year-old girl because they couldn't handle her." She wouldn't look his way, and he could see how tense she was.

"You know this how?"

"Tolly and Gail know more about the people here

and the things that go on than I realized. And I think Gail was scared for us, because she handled it. She met the woman at my place while I was over here so I wouldn't know anymore. Then there's that golden package in your bottom drawer, which has ammunition on the council about their latest escapades. I don't know exactly what, but again, Gail knew the details. There's some funding they continue to leverage for personal use with no government oversight. I'm only guessing here, but I think Gail and maybe Tolly made sure the council took a step back."

He just stared and didn't know what to say, letting out a heavy sigh. Then he lifted his beer and took a swallow. She leaned in and just sat there as he looked over to her. "As chief of this island, I'm not looking the other way, Billy Jo."

Not on Ash Byrd, and not on the council, he thought. Then there were Gail and Tolly. He didn't know how to deal with the two of them. They didn't run this island anymore, even though he was getting the feeling strings were being pulled behind his back.

He pulled a hand over his brow and glanced down to her, seeing the way she was looking up at him. She nudged him and leaned closer.

"Why would she leave her kids?" he said. Maybe out of all of it, that was the one thing that bothered him. "You think she had a choice?" He slid his arm around Billy Jo. He was still angry—no, furious.

"I don't know, Mark. I think Gail didn't want me to know anymore than I did, maybe because I told her I can't lie to you. I know it's a no-go for you. But the Sunday I met down at the ocean, who showed me who she really is, I don't think she gave a second thought to those babies. Maybe that's a good thing." She was leaning against him, and he looked down to her again. He wondered if policing this island would always come with this impossible undercurrent.

"So you don't think she'll turn up," he said.

Billy Jo sat up and slid around to face him, and he let his hand slide down her arm. "Nope, I think she's long gone. You can't help everyone, Mark, and this may sound horrible, but I, for one, am glad she's gone, because if she were still here, I would always worry she'd accuse you of the kind of sexual impropriety that would destroy you. What was already threatened could blow up on you. I'm sorry if that sounds cruel, but it's how I feel. And since I'm being totally honest here, I'm glad that Gail and Tolly have taken the lead on this and are keeping you out of the crosshairs, because there's one thing I learned long ago. A free and just society is just an illusion, and I'm not going to sit back on the sidelines and do nothing."

He really looked at her.

"You're furious with me, aren't you?" she said. When he said nothing, she swatted his thigh.

"Ow! Hey," he said, then laughed and lifted his beer.

"I just spilled everything," she said. "Sometimes you can be so damn infuriating. Say something. Are you angry with me still? What—"

He leaned down and kissed her, sliding his hand around the back of her head, tasting the wine on her lips. Then he pulled back. "Let's go in, unless you're planning on running out." He stood up and held his hand out to her, and she settled her hand in his.

"Nope, not going anywhere," she said.

He pulled her up and kissed her again just as the dog came running back and barked at the closed door, and he heard a meow from inside in reply. Billy Jo laughed, holding her wine out, and he held her against him.

A three-legged cat, a mangy mutt, and a cabin in the woods. He couldn't wait to see what tomorrow would bring.

Chapter 17

"You know, having a tattoo removed is worse than having one put on," the technician said. "The number of people who carry on and complain and whine because of how much it hurts… That's why we now numb it with anaesthesia, but there's still burning and blistering from the laser. The good news is that because of all the colored ink of this very pretty woman's face, I think you'll be sitting here for six or maybe seven more visits."

Mark was in a chair that reminded him of a dentist's office, taking in a guy with a nose ring and glasses. He had to remind himself who he was doing this for.

"Let me guess," the guy continued. "She was your wife, the one you thought you'd love forever, and you broke up?"

He wondered how often he did this and how long it took him to break clients down until they told him their stories. "One too many beers and I thought it was a good idea at the time. I'm sure you've heard it before."

Above him, on a mounted TV, the news was on.

"Can you turn that up?" he said to the guy as he lined up the laser.

The guy looked over to the TV, reached for a remote beside him, and turned it up just as the glass front door opened, and there was Billy Jo walking in. The guy glanced her way.

"My current girlfriend, if that answers your question," Mark said.

The guy made a face. "Good choice."

Billy Jo wore blue jeans that hung low on her hips, a black V-neck, and her bulky purse. Mark gestured to the stool on the other side of him and took in Billy Jo as she sat.

When two more women walked through the door, the guy called out, "Hey, I'll be right there." He turned to Mark. "Give me a few minutes to take care of them and I'll be right back. Your arm should be good and numb then, and we can start."

He wanted to tell him to take his time, as Billy Jo was now sitting on the round stool on wheels, looking at him.

"You go shopping?" he asked.

Her expression said everything. "I browsed, and now I'm done. So how long did he say it will take?"

He glanced over to his arm. His shirt was off, and he could feel the numbness now. "Apparently, I have to come back half a dozen more times."

She made a face and ran her hand over his arm.

Damn, her touch felt good. He glanced back to the TV, the news, seeing a scene in front of a west Hollywood Hills mansion with police in the background.

The reporter was saying, "Hollywood producer Mel Atwood has been found dead along with an unknown woman, but reports just coming in have confirmed that the body is that of Sunday Byrd, Atwood's girlfriend. The two were reportedly found in the house by a cleaner, shot dead, and authorities are not ruling out a break-in, suggesting it's likely they surprised a burglar."

Billy Jo was still touching him, and he thought she hissed, or maybe it was his head as he sat up from where he had been lounging in the chair, seeing the sketch of Sunday. It took him a second, as he stared at the news, the gate the reporter was standing in front of, and the police behind it, for him to know Ash had to have had a hand in this.

Billy Jo held his arm, but the shock in her expression had nothing on what he felt. "So he found her. Do you think Tolly…?"

Mark just shook his head, glancing over to the front desk, where the tattoo removal guy was still talking to the two pretty girls. He glanced back to Billy Jo and then lay back down. On the news, the byline was still running and neighbors were being interviewed.

"I don't know, Billy Jo. Seriously, she went right back to Hollywood. Do you think that was why she wanted to leave Ash, for him? I don't know what the hell to think."

"Okay, buckle up," the technician called out, heading back over. "You're ready for round one. Let's get this pretty face off." He glanced over to Billy Jo. "Not your pretty face. Bad choice of words."

Mark reached for Billy Jo's hand and said to the guy, "Well, come on. What are you waiting for? Get that tattoo off."

When he looked up to the TV again, the anchor was talking about another case, a traffic accident. For a moment, Mark wished Ash Byrd had never shown up on his island.

Billy Jo linked her fingers with his and then stood up and kissed him. "You know what? I'm going to buy you a gift for lying there and doing this for me."

"What kind of gift?" he said to her, knowing the guy was listening.

"Oh, the kind that's short, black, and silky—and there might be some lace," she said, then ran her hand down his leg and lifted it in a wave before she strode to the front door.

"Wow, I bet you can't wait to see that sexy number," the guy said.

Mark shot him a look. "Just take the tattoo off," he said.

He dragged his gaze back over to the TV, seeing the image of Sunday again beside producer Mel Atwood, a man in his fifties. All he could wonder was what the hell was wrong with that picture. It sickened him, but he remembered what Sunday had said, that the Hollywood elites hired Ash to handle problems, and every one of them had looked at her and wanted her.

Things really did go on behind closed doors that no one knew about. When he got back to the island, his first order of business would be to make a point of finding out what secrets everyone who lived there was hiding.

And Billy Jo? Well, he really was going to enjoy her gift, her smile, and the fact that he rather liked her next to him.

He listened to the whir of the laser, the sound of the traffic. When they got home, he'd tell her how much he loved her.

Epilogue

At least the rain had stopped.

The surrounding darkness would have bothered anyone else, but Ash welcomed it. A darkened road was ideal, with its canopy of trees barely revealing the moonlight through the clouds that had gathered a few days earlier. He heard footsteps in the gravel, and a light popped on inside his car as the passenger door opened and Tolly Shephard climbed in with a swoosh of the leather seat.

He pulled the door closed. "So who's watching your kids?"

Not what Ash had been expecting Tolly to ask. He'd told the former police chief where to meet him at the end of Anderson, an unpaved private road that went nowhere and backed onto a hundred acres of parkland. The only cars that ever came out there were filled with teenagers looking for a place to hang out, party, drink, and do the typical teenage stuff that parents on the island had no idea their kids were doing.

"The nanny I hired," Ash replied.

Suzette was over from Australia on a student visa, but her papers had expired, and she'd been looking for a job at his hotel. She said she'd come from a big family, a redhead with a sweet smile, short and boxy, twenty-three. Ash lifted the thick envelope on the centre console between the seats and handed it to Tolly, who hesitated only a second before taking it.

"Includes a bonus," Ash said. He knew Tolly wouldn't count it, one hundred thousand that would never be traced.

"You kill her?" Tolly said as he thumbed through the stacks of cash in the envelope.

He'd known Tolly Shephard a long time, enough to know he was a very smart man. "You know why you kept your job as long as you did?" he said.

Tolly never smiled. He dragged his gaze over to Ash in the darkness, but Ash could still see something in his expression though it was pitch black. "Figured it was because I didn't look too hard into what you were doing."

"Oh, come on, Tolly. You know this would be political suicide for you. I'm too close with the people who pay your salary…"

"I'm very well aware of everything you do, Ash, so let's not dance around it. I know you were the guy in the background of the last state governor election. You worked the scene and had the ear of every news correspondent. They were in your pocket. You told them where to focus their stories, which headlines to use, and when it went sideways because the governor didn't do what you told him and the media was getting wind, you send in a decoy, some nutjob bussed in to discredit the angry protestors with legitimate concerns. You worked it well, encouraging the journalists to take photos of every protestor there, and then what happened? Those angry citizens became a problem and found themselves in a database of people likely to cause civil unrest. This island has to be a sideshow for you, because handling the council is not on the scale of projects you usually manage."

The way Tolly said it, Ash heard the edge in his voice. He wondered when too much would happen and Tolly would do something he shouldn't, just like the moms and pops who had shown up at protests only to find his decoys planted right beside them, screaming louder and changing the narrative. He knew exactly how to turn legitimate outrage over government abuse into annoyance at just another nutjob.

"You're right that this island is small," Ash said, "but it requires the same handholding, and whether you believe it or not, I do believe in the separation of state and media."

Tolly shook his head. "That's an odd thing for you to say, considering what you do."

What was he supposed to say? Business was business. He handled problems. Freedom was something he'd believed in when he was young and idealistic, until the unforgettable day he learned otherwise.

"Not so odd," he said. "I learned a valuable lesson one day when I was twenty and stupid, when a corporate giant took my mother's house and the bank allowed it to happen. The DA and the police were all contacted about the fraud, as the documents were backdated and the signatures forged, but the DA said he wouldn't prosecute because it wasn't in the public interest to prosecute someone that powerful. I demanded the evidence, the paper trail, and I was denied. But I'm not being denied anymore."

And Olgar Rheinsmith, the head of the corporate giant, was now facing a human rights tribunal. Not what he'd planned, but he'd take the payback.

Tolly pulled in a breath, still sitting in the car. "You didn't answer me on whether you killed her. You know Gail disabled the GPS, and Sunday turned off the cameras in the house, but the new identity Amy Holt set up for her was left in the garbage at a train station in Chicago. You knew she'd show up in California?"

He stared out the window, thinking of how he'd once saved the ass of the big Hollywood producer Sunday had left him for. He'd helped Mel Atwood out of a jam that would have ended his career, with him in his fifties, liking young girls—and then there was his wife.

"Mel Atwood was a dog," he said. "He hired me once, and I investigated the allegations against him and made them go away. He had a thing for Sunday, and she was always looking for the better catch."

He'd have forgiven anything except betrayal.

Sunday had known too many of his secrets. She'd even made a call to the Feds. At least she couldn't talk anymore.

"She was only sixteen, Ash…"

"You know she was the type of woman who feeds off the mental, physical, and material means of a man and then leaves him for dead. You think I didn't know how dangerous she was? Her parents did, too, and that's why they brought her to me, but sometimes you just can't save someone. Nothing will come back on you, Tolly. Your hands are clean."

Tolly let out a rude noise. "The mother of your children is dead. Of course I have blood on my hands. But now you'll leave Mark alone."

Ash inhaled as he thought of the redheaded chief. He didn't like wildcards because they were unpredictable, and unpredictable could be a problem for him. "You know, Tolly, I never knew you had such a soft spot for the young detective, considering what a thorn in your side he was. When Sunday showed up at his house, I think that snippy little social worker being there foiled whatever plan she had. I think she really got off on it, showing up the way she did. To her, it was a game, as if she was daring me to do something." He took in the headlights of a small car coming that way, then the loud thumping of music as it drove past.

"I mean it, Ash," Tolly said. "I found the girl. It wasn't hard. And Gail did her part, too. Now you leave Mark alone. You know you owe me, and it's all I'm asking."

He didn't understand why Tolly was so fond of Mark Friessen, but he'd stopped wondering long ago why people did the things they did. "You keep him out of my business," he said.

Tolly pulled on the door, and the inside light flicked on again. "Just don't do anything here that will have him looking your way. Mark can't be bought, and he doesn't give in to blackmail or strong-arming. He's not like who you're used to dealing with. You keep it off the island, Ash, and I mean it: Mark stays off your radar."

He just stared at Tolly, who was about to leave. "Then you make sure he stops looking into me. You know he is."

Tolly said nothing, just nodded as he climbed out.

Ash started his car, thinking of the nanny at home, watching his kids, the mother they'd never know, and the fact that Tolly and Gail Shephard had a lot more to lose than he did.

Turn the page for a sneak peek of
THE CHILDREN the next book in the *BILLY JO MCCABE MYSTERY*
Available in print, eBook & audio

She picked up the wrong file, and now everything is falling apart.

From *New York Times* & *USA Today* bestselling author Lorhainne Eckhart comes a new Billy Jo McCabe mystery set on a small island in the Pacific Northwest. When social worker Billy Jo McCabe accidentally picks up the wrong file, she discovers a shocking, twisted mystery plotted by a high-ranking social worker in the DCFS.

When Billy Jo McCabe accidentally picks up the wrong file, before she realizes her mistake, she discovers a secret no one was supposed to find.

She takes the file to the newly appointed chief of police, Mark Friessen, but he doesn't believe her—that is, until they discover dozens more files and missing money from vulnerable at-risk children who have aged out of the system and are living on the streets.

As she digs into the files, the system, and the people involved, everything falls apart.

And what Mark and Billy Jo discover is a secret far more shocking than missing money.

"Pam, I need the Gillespie file. Can you grab it for me?" Billy Jo said as she finished scribbling her notes. When she realized she hadn't heard anything in reply, she looked over to the open door of her office and leaned back in her chair, her laptop open, listening, expecting to hear footsteps, but she heard nothing.

"Pam..." she called out again, scooting her chair way back, looking to the darkened hallway, really listening. But it was quiet.

Too quiet.

She pushed back her chair and stepped into the dimly lit hall to see a darkened front door and no Pam. When she pulled back the sleeve of her navy shirt and looked at her watch, it was only ten after four.

"You couldn't even tell me you were leaving?" she muttered. Pam didn't report to her, but wasn't it a matter of courtesy?

Billy Jo walked over to the file cabinet and pulled open the second drawer, where she knew "G" was halfway down, seeing how packed full it was with paper and files, every one of them signifying a child and family in trouble.

"Gillespie, where are you?" She spotted the thick labeled file and pulled it out, realizing another file had been stuck inside it. She walked the bundle over to Pam's cleared-off desk and opened it to see a stack of papers, with notes written on the inside of the folder, as well.

She pulled out the inside file and spotted "Rae, Deena" scribbled in pen on the tab, and she found herself really looking at all the notes by Link Stone, an older social worker from a year ago or maybe earlier—notes and numbers, with what looked like dollar amounts listed:

$2,384

$1,177

$129

$4,584

She didn't have a clue what any of it meant.

She flicked her gaze to the Gillespie file and then back to the Rae file before unfolding a thick piece of paper from the latter. An envelope slipped out and fell to the industrial gray carpet. She bent down and picked it up.

"What is this?" She took in the folded envelope with "Link Stone" scribbled messily in pencil on the front. It was unsealed, so she opened it and found a check inside, the kind of state check she was familiar with.

The amount of $834 was made out to Deena Rae, and from the color of the check and the date, she knew it was from over a year earlier. "Who is Deena Rae?" she said, recalling the file had been tucked inside the Gillespie file. She flipped the check over again to see that Deena Rae had in turn signed it over to Link Stone.

What the hell?

Billy Jo looked up and over to the tinted industrial windows. This seemed both off and wrong. When her cell phone started ringing, she glanced over her shoulder to her office but turned back to the file, to the check she was holding. She flipped through the pages of notes, looking for an intake form or something, her brow furrowing. There was a photo: dark hair, Hispanic, she thought, and not very old, maybe early teens, with the same haunted mugshot expression she was familiar with.

"Now, why is a check for Deena Rae signed over to you, Link…?"

The locked front door rattled, and then came a pounding. Her cell phone was ringing again, too. She looked over to see her guy on the other side of the door. Mark wore a jean jacket and blue jeans, and damn, did he look good. Check in hand, she strode to the door in her sandals and faded jeans and flicked open the lock.

He pulled the door open, and her heart did a flip-flop. "You didn't answer," he said.

"Sorry, was trying to figure out a mystery." She held up the check and took in his frown in reply. Was this that feeling everyone talked about, that honeymoon phase, where she wanted to spend every second around him?

His gaze lingered, and she wondered if he knew what she was thinking. He reached for the check and really looked at it, turning it over. It was the cop in him that made him too perfect for her. "What is this?"

She started walking, feeling him right behind her, so close. His hand slid over her back as she neared Pam's desk. "I was looking for a file and found this one tucked inside it, for a Deena Rae, whom I've never seen before. That check was in this envelope. Not sure why it was signed over to Link Stone. He was a social worker here a year ago, maybe, I think."

His hand fell away, but he was standing so close to her, looking over her at the file. She didn't need to touch him because there was barely an inch between them, just like when they were sleeping. She never would have believed sleeping next to someone would be something she could get used to.

"I take it this is unusual?" he said. Damn, he was handsome when he was trying to figure something out. This was the man she could see herself with forever.

"Yeah. I mean, what is this check even for? Deena Rae… I'm thinking this is her photo. Young, by the looks of it, and she signed over a check. Why? It hasn't been cashed."

"You know, Billy Jo, it could be for a dozen

reasons. Maybe she didn't have a bank account. You found it in the file?"

She nodded. "Yup, tucked in an envelope right here, with Link's name on it. I don't know, Mark. That doesn't make sense. If a youth is getting a check from the state, she doesn't sign it over to a social worker."

Mark was holding the check back out to her, and she could see he was done with the topic as he glanced to the door and back to her. "You almost finished? I want to grab some dinner. Carmen's on tonight, so thought we'd do a steak and then head home."

And that was it. He wasn't going to ask anything else.

She tucked the check back in the envelope and closed up the file. "Yeah, I'm done. So that's it?"

He seemed distracted. "I'm hungry," he said. "It's a check. You're sure it wasn't cashed?"

Her brow knit. "Yeah," she said. "This is odd."

He let out a sigh. "Look, you said he hasn't worked here in how long? So an uncashed check is stuck in a file. Seems like bureaucracy at its finest. I'm sure there's an explanation, Billy Jo, that doesn't involve us standing here, trying to figure out something that likely happened long ago. Maybe a new check was issued, or maybe it was a mistake. But the last thing I want to do after the day I've had is get tied up in some wild goose chase. Please let's go eat."

She was about to argue with him, and she wondered if that was why he pulled her close, right against him, and then leaned down and kissed her. She entwined her arms around his neck when he pulled back, appearing distracted.

"You okay?" she said. "Something happen today?"

He stepped back, which was also unlike him, and a shadow flickered across his expression. "Just the stress of being chief on an island where it seems like I'm constantly wading into a minefield of politics run rampant. Just once, you know, I'd like to not have to wonder what kind of bullshit is going to come out of the closet." He ran his hand over the back of his neck. He really was not having a good day.

"Council still giving you problems?"

"Seems they're always doing something—but, believe it or not, today it's not them. Seems the state has suddenly flagged Carmen as a homegrown terrorist." He wasn't smiling.

She waited for the teasing, but his pissed-off expression remained in place. "Carmen, our Carmen?"

He angled his head. "My reaction exactly. I spent the rest of the day on the phone, being sent from one career politician to the next as each agency said it wasn't their department. I finally called the Feds, talked with an Agent Kruger in the Seattle office. Seems Carmen Zarko is a common name. I expected him to say he'd fix it, but guess what? It's not that simple."

She knew she was frowning. "And how did you find this out?"

He brushed back his jean jacket as he rested his hands on his hips, those hands that stirred so much in her, and she took in his holstered gun, his badge. "Well, funny thing. I convinced Carmen to take some time off, so she called her sister—you know, the one who has her kid? She worked something out and was going to fly down there, but she went to book her ticket and her name was flagged. She walked into my office, and I've never seen that look on her face before. I told her there had to be an explanation. It seems someone flagged her even though the Carmen Zarko who's supposed to be on the list is a different Carmen, ten years older, and lives in Ecuador, part of some militia. All I got was runaround after runaround, from 'It's not my department,' to 'Sorry, I understand your frustration,' to 'Submit a request in writing to the state department.' But, as the agent I was talking to said, I'll need good luck, because Carmen has a better chance of winning the lottery than getting this fixed." He let out a heavy sigh.

"So…" she started.

"So I told her to take an extra few days and drive. She told me thanks for trying. You know, sometimes, Billy Jo, the incompetence amazes me."

She ran her hand over his arm. "So steak it is," she said. At least now she knew why he wasn't interested in helping her with this mystery.

"And your company," he said as she slid her hands over his shoulders again, feeling how tight he was. He pulled her closer and patted her bottom. "You ready?"

She still needed to figure out why a signed check for Deena Rae was in that file. Then there was the Gillespie file and the paperwork she needed to finish. "Let me just grab my purse and my phone."

He had that brooding look. She knew he was there for everyone. She kissed him again and then stepped away, starting back to the office, before she turned back to him.

"You know, Mark, you can do only what you can do."

He let his gaze linger. "That doesn't make me feel any better," he said. He looked over to the open files she had left on Pam's desk, files she planned to dig into, but tonight she needed to be there for Mark with dinner and a backrub. Tomorrow, she'd figure out what the story was with Deena Rae and the social worker, Link Stone. Opening that file had thrown her into another mystery she knew she wouldn't be able to turn away from.

She grabbed her purse and sweater and tucked her phone inside her bag. When she stepped out of the office, there was her quiet, brooding Mark, holding the check, looking at the file. All she could think of was something her mom had said, that sometimes you had to put aside your own worries to be there for someone you loved.

About the Author

"Lorhainne Eckhart is one of my go to authors when I want a guaranteed good book. So many twists and turns, but also so much love and such a strong sense of family."

(Lora W., Reviewer)

New York Times & USA Today bestseller Lorhainne Eckhart writes Raw Relatable Real Romance is best known for her big family romances series, where "Morals and family are running themes. Danger, romance, and a drive to do what is right will see you glued to the page." As one fan calls her, she is the "Queen of the family saga." (aherman) writing "the ups and downs of what goes on within a family but also with some suspense, angst and of course a bit of romance thrown in for good measure." Follow Lorhainne on Bookbub to receive alerts on New Releases and Sales and join her mailing list at LorhainneEckhart.com for her Monday Blog, books news, giveaways and **FREE** reads. With over 120 books, audiobooks, and multiple series published and available at all retailers now translated into six languages. She is a multiple recipient of the Readers' Favorite Award for Suspense and Romance, and lives in the Pacific Northwest on an island, is the mother of three, her oldest has autism and she is an advocate for never giving up on your dreams.

"Lorhainne Eckhart has this uncanny way of just hitting the spot every time with her books."

(Caroline L., Reviewer)

The O'Connells: *The O'Connells of Livingston, Montana are not your typical family. A riveting collection of stories surrounding the ups and downs of what goes on within a family but also with some suspense, angst and of course a bit of romance thrown in for good measure "I thought I loved the Friessens, but I abso-*

lutely adore the O'Connell's. Each and
every book has totally different genres of
stories but the one thing in common is
how she is able to wrap it around the
family which is the heart of each story."
(C. Logue)

The Friessens: An emotional big family
romance series, the Friessen family
siblings find their relationships tested, lay
their hearts on the line, and discover
lasting love! "Lorhainne Eckhart is one of
my go to authors when I want a guaranteed good book. So many twists and turns,
but also so much love and such a strong
sense of family." (Lora W., Reviewer)

The Parker Sisters: The Parker Sisters
are a close-knit family, and like any other
family they have their ups and downs.
"Eckhart has crafted another intense
family drama…The character develop-
ment is outstanding, and the emotional
investment is high…" (Aherman,
Reviewer)

The McCabe Brothers: Join the five
McCabe siblings on their journeys to the
dark and dangerous side of love! An
intense, exhilarating collection of romantic
thrillers you won't want to miss. —

"Eckhart has a new series that is defi-nitely worth the read. The queen of the family saga started this series with a spin-off of her wildly successful Friessen series." From a Readers' Favorite award —winning author and "queen of the family saga" (Aherman)

Lorhainne loves to hear from her readers! You can connect with me at:

www.LorhainneEckhart.com
lorhainneeckhart.le@gmail.com

Also by Lorhainne Eckhart

The Outsider Series
The Forgotten Child (Brad and Emily)
A Baby and a Wedding *(An Outsider Series Short)*
Fallen Hero (Andy, Jed, and Diana)
The Search *(An Outsider Series Short)*
The Awakening (Andy and Laura)
Secrets (Jed and Diana)
Runaway (Andy and Laura)
Overdue *(An Outsider Series Short)*
The Unexpected Storm (Neil and Candy)
The Wedding (Neil and Candy)

The Friessens: A New Beginning
The Deadline (Andy and Laura)
The Price to Love (Neil and Candy)
A Different Kind of Love (Brad and Emily)
A Vow of Love, A Friessen Family Christmas

The Friessens
The Reunion
The Bloodline (Andy & Laura)
The Promise (Diana & Jed)
The Business Plan (Neil & Candy)
The Decision (Brad & Emily)
First Love (Katy)
Family First

Leave the Light On
In the Moment
In the Family
In the Silence
In the Charm
Unexpected Consequences
It Was Always You
The First Time I Saw You
Welcome to My Arms
Welcome to Boston
I'll Always Love You
Ground Rules
A Reason to Breathe
You Are My Everything
Anything For You
The Homecoming
Stay Away From My Daughter
The Bad Boy
A Place of Our Own
The Visitor
All About Devon
Long Past Dawn
How to Heal a Heart
Keep Me In Your Heart

The O'Connells
The Neighbor
The Third Call
The Secret Husband
The Quiet Day
The Commitment

The Missing Father
The Hometown Hero
Justice
The Family Secret
The Fallen O'Connell
The Return of the O'Connells
And The She Was Gone
The Stalker
The O'Connell Family Christmas
The Girl Next Door
Broken Promises
The Gatekeeper

The McCabe Brothers
Don't Stop Me (Vic)
Don't Catch Me (Chase)
Don't Run From Me (Aaron)
Don't Hide From Me (Luc)
Don't Leave Me (Claudia)
Out of Time

A Billy Jo McCabe Mystery
Nothing As it Seems
Hiding in Plain Sight
The Cold Case
The Trap
Above the Law
The Stranger at the Door
The Children
The Last Stand

The Street Fighter
Finding Home

The Wilde Brothers
The One (Joe and Margaret)
The Honeymoon, A Wilde Brothers Short
Friendly Fire (Logan and Julia)
Not Quite Married, A Wilde Brothers Short
A Matter of Trust (Ben and Carrie)
The Reckoning, A Wilde Brothers Christmas
Traded (Jake)
Unforgiven (Samuel)
The Holiday Bride

Married in Montana
His Promise
Love's Promise
A Promise of Forever

The Parker Sisters
Thrill of the Chase
The Dating Game
Play Hard to Get
What We Can't Have
Go Your Own Way
A June Wedding

Kate & Walker
One Night
Edge of Night
Last Night

Walk the Right Road Series
The Choice
Lost and Found
Merkaba
Bounty
Blown Away: The Final Chapter

The Saved Series
Saved
Vanished
Captured

Single Titles
He Came Back
Loving Christine

For my German Readers
Die Außenseiter-Reihe
Der Vergessene Junge
Der Gefallene Held

For my French Readers
L'ENFANT OUBLIÉ